T0286945

Gravity

First published in 2022
by the Black Spring Press Group
from the Eyewear Publishing imprint
Grantully Road, Maida Vale, London W9,
United Kingdom

Cover design and typeset by Edwin Smet
Author photograph Charles R. Lucke

The right of Judith Serin to be identified as author of
this work has been asserted in accordance with section 77
of the Copyright, Designs and Patents Act 1988

*Editor's note: the author has requested
that American spelling and grammar be used in this work.*

ISBN 978-1-913606-36-7

THE **BLACK SPRING**
PRESS GROUP

BLACKSPRINGPRESSGROUP.COM

Judith Serin

Gravity

Six stories and a novella
about women

In memory of my sister Joan Serin
and my husband Herbert Yee

CONTENTS

MAIL

The mailman walks across the street with an offering. It's not for me. I don't get mail anymore. I took down my mailbox. I wanted to flatten it like an aluminum beer can, one step and it pops. I couldn't. It was perfectly unyielding. I kicked it and stubbed my toe. It clattered down the front steps knocking over a jar with an angel-winged begonia that I was rooting for my sister. "Oh fuck you," I shouted.

My neighbor Joe came to the doorway of the cottage behind. He's a carpenter. We finished the job with his sledgehammer, and he gave me a glass of root beer with lemon squeezed in it. He's used to me.

It was easier than I thought to stop getting mail. They may have tried to call, but I wasn't answering the phone. A man from the post office finally came by. "Oh, she's moved," I explained, trying to look like a healthy young wife. "We're knocking down the partition, making the place into one apartment. For the baby, you know." I smiled complacently. Healthy young wives think having a baby is such an accomplishment. "No, she didn't leave her new address. I think she was moving to Australia."

That may have been a bit much, but the post office man left. I guess he gave up.

So you can't send me mail. There's no possibility I'll receive a letter with a bomb in it. I could send you one, I suppose, but I'm afraid of the authorities. Remember how frightened I was before that flight to Bermuda, the one vacation you took me on? You probably thought I was afraid of the airplane. You looked smug, as usual. You love it when I'm scared of things; it makes you feel superior. Well, go ahead; you have little enough to feel superior about. At least you can be proud that you're too dumb for neuroses. Anyway, I wasn't scared of the airplane. I was terrified of the metal detector. All those officials with guns standing around, the mysterious machine that surely isn't infallible. Suppose it discovers I have silver lungs or a platinum uterus? They'd search my pockets, remove my clothes. They'd have to take me apart. Once accused, I'll confess to anything, you know that. I'd tell them, no matter how irrelevant, about my undeclared income in the last year of school; the bill I never paid when I moved from Vermont; the marijuana I smoked — especially if they have guns or black ties.

You took advantage of this. You really did. When anything went wrong, you blamed me. You knew I believed you no matter how vigorously I defended myself. You asked me if I read your mail because you knew I couldn't lie. You can lie. You did it constantly with such ease I began to believe that you were simple-minded and didn't remember the truth. When I did something wrong, you waited. You knew I'd tell you. I saw your self-satisfied look. He's waiting for me to tell him, I thought, and did. Then you exploded in simulated hurt surprise.

I'd gladly send you a bomb in a letter. I'd gladly send you a big bomb in a parcel post package, except that I'm afraid of the authorities. They'd find me. The cracks in the sidewalk would lead them to me. They'd tape-record my voice and hear the fear in my breath. The color of my eyes would change when they mentioned your name. Through them they would see my brain exploding again and again with you at the center.

I won't send you a bomb because the police and FBI agents can take an airplane across the country or even drive gathering evidence along the way in all those rectangular states I've never been to. But you can't take an airplane either. You could never take time off, even for a weekend in Vermont. And if you could, you wouldn't find me without a mailbox and my telephone turned off. Would you come here, walking the streets, looking for me? You don't need glasses, but you're too dumb to read the cracks in the sidewalk. You can't get sick; your blood is too thick for germs to live there. You can't even hear the messages from your poor body, suffering on the cross of your cruel mind, which won't listen to anyone. Still,

you might walk on the streets and look for me.
Well, I'm not worried. I'm more practical
than you think; I can plan. If you come to town,
I'll know. I have spies. A woman walks past my
window every morning wearing a beige raincoat
and a blue knit cap, even when it's sunny. That
cap knows me; it looks out for you. It's efficient; it
sees everything in 360 degrees. It travels with the
woman to the central bus station to ride into the
city. All newcomers must pass through there as
through a metal detector. It watches for signs of
you. The crumpled brown candy wrapper on the
aqua linoleum; the balls of dust in the corners of
long benches; tumbleweed blown by the wind of
your malice.

I have a dog spy too, a small dirty one with
sharp white teeth that will nip your ankles. All
his fleas are watching. He trots around town,
visits every breakfast cafe, waits by the door for
blue-suited businessmen with donut crumbs
on their lapels. When you come here — bleary
from the late flight, a little heavier from all that
distance — you will want coffee. No cafe is safe
for you. You'll sit down bending over to sip the

first too hot mouthful from the too full cup. You'll shuffle your big feet under the table to find a berth for them. Then those sharp little teeth, the blood on the ankle, the alarm sounded.

Other spies stalk the town for me. You won't know them. I will only tell you that there are many caterpillars here and many birds.

When you come, we'll take action. The whole town will turn against you. This town is my friend. I know you won't believe me. You think I can't make friends; that I'm too sensitive, too quiet; why don't I talk to people? I don't need to talk to this town. It lets me walk on its streets, buy an ice cream cone, admire its flowers and sunsets, all with a minimum of words and gestures. It will grow barricades to stop you: huge concrete barrels in a line across the street. The plum trees will drop their fruit on the sidewalk. You'll slip, covering your round-toed shoes in slime, staining your tweed trousers, landing on your ass in a pile of skin and seeds.

You'll walk on the fault and you won't know it's there until the sidewalk rumbles and opens under your feet. On Point Reyes in 1906, a crack opened under a cow and she fell in. It closed over her, but her tail stuck out. The dogs ate it. This may happen to you. I can't decide which I'd rather leave in the air — your stupid surprised head, choking with swollen tongue extended, or your slippery heel as you struggle in the suffocating soil, the earthworms and centipedes approaching.

So don't try to come after me because I haven't committed suicide yet. I know you're disappointed. You were so sure I couldn't live without you. You've been checking your computer for news from the West. Waiting for a small story with my name. You won't see it. With you I was always standing on chairs on top of couches, reaching for a light bulb a little farther than my arm. I walked on decks of skyscrapers in the wind, my hat blowing off. Subway doors closed between us. There are trap doors in the long well-light halls without windows. Any word of mine might trigger them.

Now I stand here with my feet firm on the faulted earth, and the hazy sky folds around me. I'm safe, encased in a new metal unknown to East Coast man. But don't think this is forever. Don't believe you'll get away with only a draw. With dropping it. With time to make us forget until it's a tiny scar on the thumb — a twinge in the bone on rainy days. No. We'll meet again when I'm ready.

Someday we'll be stranded on a desert island. I'll stab you with a sharp stick. You'll die slowly while I dance around you, singing songs you hate. I'll eat your flesh, roasting it over a pretty wood fire, seasoning it with leaves and flowers to cover the bitter taste. It will keep me till my ship comes in.

A TREASURE

Dear Julie,

I've purchased a young man. It was purely on impulse. You know I usually don't go in for that sort of extravagance. Before this, I never understood why a woman would want one.

I saw him in a shop window a couple of weeks ago. The weather had just turned to fall, snapped into it overnight. You know how these seasonal changes stir you and arouse old feelings of longing from a time when you still believed your life was susceptible to sudden shifts and magical solutions? So I was walking more slowly than usual, dawdling, waiting for some shape to emerge from the gray of the city's streets. I noticed him in one of those awful glittering window displays — all mirrors and fake snow. He was seated in an elaborate papier-mâché sled: swan-shaped and drawn by four impossibly delicate horses. He leaned his elbows on its rococo wing, his chin in his hand. He had a watchfulness that matched my own. A sign in the corner of the window announced, "SALE."

I thought only my curiosity was aroused. I called to a salesman lounging in the doorway, "How come he's on sale? Is he sick?"

"Oh no," the fellow replied in a tone that managed to be both obsequious and unfriendly. "He's last season's model; we're making room for the new look."

"Why didn't anyone buy him?"

"Not good looking enough, I guess." The salesman shrugged.

Not good looking! I turned toward the boy, who gazed back at me with a hint of interest. My longing crystallized. He was lovely, perfect, a treasure. Oh, not all blond and cold and muscular, like those little animals sopranos parade at parties. He was round-faced and brown-eyed and held himself with an unselfconscious grace. And the hair — the perfect short curls, like a poodle, like a child's stuffed toy.

The salesman sensed my shift. "I can give him to you for ten percent off. He's in very good condition."

"Ten percent!" I knew I must bargain coldly, hide my new-born desire. "Last season's look. I can't go anywhere with him. I'd only buy him out of charity."

I argued the salesman down to half price, while the boy flushed. Poor thing, I thought. This hurts his pride. I'll console him when we get home.

Well, Julie, I didn't console him. I took him to the bedroom and he curled up and went to sleep. I sat there watching him. He wheezed a little — probably has allergies. When I reached to touch his hair, he turned his head away.

He isn't trained. I thought they were taught what to do, but he doesn't do anything. And he doesn't speak the language. When I talk to him, he shakes his head politely. I've heard him murmuring to the cats in some indefinable tongue. I tried to teach him my name, hoping he would reveal his in return. I settled on the blue couch next to him. "Carla," I enunciated pointing at myself, "Car-la." He watched courteously. He didn't repeat after me or offer any word in his own language. I said "Carla," poking my chest, at least twenty times. My strained smile made the corners of my mouth ache. When my hands fell to my lap in defeat, he sprang up and returned to the bedroom, where he finished sketching the fish in my aquarium. The drawings are accurate and elegant.

Julie, I can hear your indignant voice, "It's an outrage. Take him back. Haul that unscrupulous salesman into court..." But I can't. I feel sheepish writing this, but I'm in love with him. I can't think of being without him.

The strange thing is that I'm getting nothing out of it. These purchases are supposed to provide convenient, docile pleasure. I don't even dare to touch mine. I know I should start something myself, but the first time I tried, he pulled out of my arms. I'm frightened of feeling that pain again, like a wall of water knocking my breath away.

I wait stupidly for a change. Do I expect him

to wake me one morning with a kiss and declare his love for me in a charming accent? I follow him around the apartment. I've begun biting my lips; they're always engorged with blood. It hurts to be here. But it hurts even more to be away. I'm impatient on my way home. I imagine that he has escaped through the kitchen window — he sits by it for hours — or worse, that when I am gone, he is happy, animated, smiles.

He doesn't smile. He looks thoughtful, slightly anxious. Afraid, perhaps, that I'll pounce on him though I always hold myself back. I see him now through the doorway, seated at the kitchen table, examining my collection of stones. His round, solemn face is in semi-darkness; it emerges from the jungle of his incongruous curls. I notice his lips which look soft like a pale peeled fruit, his short thick fingers. He's wearing the wine-red sweater I bought him. Its high collar hugging his neck. I feel so tender toward that sweater. I want to be where it is now: hands and breasts and arms against his skin, wrapping him, suffocating him with warmth.

Well, Julie, please write. How's your garden? I think about last July — the tomatoes we planted must be ripe now.

Love,

Carla

WOMEN AND MEN I: THE MILITARY MAN

I seem to be living with an older military man. I don't know how it happened. He wears boots all the time, even in bed. He has silver hair and looks a bit like my first psychiatrist but so much shinier with all the buttons and medals. Dr. Wheeler was tweedy.

The military man isn't unkind. Sort of distant, like an uncle who mixes you up with your sister and has no idea what to get you for your birthday. He wants his coffee early in the morning, in the study. The window gleams behind him when I bring it in. He's already at his desk but hasn't turned on the light. In a few minutes the sun will rise: no need to waste electricity.

I never see him lying down, only feel him in the dark. He's always up and dressed before dawn, up and dressed after I'm asleep. He doesn't read in bed. He changes in his own little bedroom. When he comes in the dark to the big bed and wakes me, it could be a trusted master sergeant. His chest is large and heavy and colder than the wisps of my evaporating dreams.

He is away most of the day. Perhaps not away, but in a distant room in this military building. There are innumerable rooms, many with windows behind desks. In places it is a graceful military mansion: the bedroom with a tall four-poster, white silk sheets, and a lace canopy; the kitchens with huge pantries and jolly male cooks, who seem so friendly but will never talk to me beyond an obsequious, "Yes, Miss. No, Miss." Sometimes it is a military skyscraper: thousands of offices, each floor with a different colored carpet. Below, I know, is the New York pavement, a suicide's heaven.

The military man wears gloves and encourages me to do likewise. He takes me to luncheon. He appears. "Put on your gloves; I'm taking you to luncheon." Very plush red chairs. We are the only ones in the restaurant or club. I'm sure it's not a dining room; there are menus and a waiter. The other members of our party are also military men. They look older than mine, less handsome and precise. They have bulbous noses, big bellies, thinning hair. I would run away with any of them, but they speak to me only at the beginning and end of the meals. When they are with us, it is especially hard to keep gravy off my gloves, my white dress.

What do we talk about, me and my military man? Difficult to remember, even seconds after he has kissed me and strode out of the room. My clothes? "Try a ribbon on your hat," he says. "I'll bring you one this evening." I question him about his friends at luncheon. He has trouble recognizing them from my descriptions. I say the one with the bald spot and large red ears. He says the one discussing strategic withholding devices. I ask what they think of me. "Oh, they all like you." Why, I wonder.

I don't know what I'm supposed to do here. Maybe arrange flowers. In the room outside my bedroom there are flowers every morning: cut, laid out on the table, their long stems toward me. In the evening I want to see them lying there dead. I imagine brown curling the edge of a lily; carnations withered to a clenched fist; sticks of thorns, rose petals littering the carpet. But, when I pass through the room on the way to my night-time shower, they're gone.

Once, I tried to check on the flowers at noon. Maybe there would be someone arranging them — a maid, another woman. I couldn't find my way back. I got lost in corridors, turning corners. Clerks with glasses and felt ties opened every door when I collapsed on the pea-green carpet, crying.

WOMEN AND MEN II: DESTROYING THE WORLD

I love the man I'm living with but he's destroying the world. He drives everywhere. He never recycles. He uses products tested on animals. I tell him his convenience isn't worth these things, but he won't listen. He has a look of resolute non-listening whenever I bring the subject up.

Recently I've been seeing landscapes when we make love. They just pop into my mind slipping between my eyelids and a thought in the pigeonhole center of my brain about what bills we can afford to pay this month. Once I saw an orchard — old, overgrown. The trees full of small green fruit. Then the leaves fell all at once with a whooshing sound, like a barn catching fire. The fruit dropped, smashing on the ground. The trees uprooted themselves, groaning, toppling slowly onto their sides.

Another time it was a human landscape. Everything was brown. People huddled in the evening light, their arms hugging their knees. Each was about ten feet from her or his neighbor on the coppery bare earth. They were in perfect rows like newly planted sprouts. One began to dig. Soon they all were digging, scratching in the hard soil like dogs. Occasionally someone found a stone and held it for a moment. I felt the cool bulge in my hand. Then the digger would toss it a few feet away. The holes deepened. Haphazard walls formed around each person. The pace of work accelerated; people panted and sighed. When the moon rose in the russet sky, they flung themselves headfirst into their holes.

Once I saw a landscape of chickens. Millions of white hens and roosters screeched in alarm, trying to climb on top of each other in their impossible attempts to escape since they filled the world to the horizon. So many chickens were somehow alarming. I began to worry that their hysterical attention might be turned toward me. But they continued struggling among themselves, an enormous feather pillow straining to come apart. Then waves of heat rose from their backs. Their feathers wilted and dropped. They turned yellow, crusty brown, steaming.

I find these visions somehow exciting. They support rather than distract from sex. But there is still the question of what to do about this man I love. He must be taught. I must break through his nonchalance. Should I leave him, hurting myself as much as I hurt him? Or should I keep on trying to bring him to his senses, talking and talking while he looks into the mirror?

RELEASING

I knew I would have to split up with him and it broke my heart. He was so innocent, so unconscious when he hurt me. Like a child, a beautiful boy who was sure the world loved him. Whenever I complained, his brown eyes, ringed with luxuriant lashes, would gaze straight into mine, the hair that matched his eyes falling in a thick fringe across his high forehead. He'd smile and plead confidently, sure of being forgiven. "But Cynthia, I was just a little late; I lost track of time." And I would smile back — the long drive in rush hour; the laundry piling up; the strain of leaving work early to make the movie, his movie, that he wanted me to see all beating behind my eyes. But a part of my brain forgave him in his childlike incompetence, his sweetness.

I always forgave him. I was too tired to get angry. It was futile. He didn't mean to be unkind. Why ruin what pleasure I could still get from the evening? And I loved him.

It was Sophie's call that Saturday morning that convinced me. Sophie was his mother, casual, hip, far too sharp and sophisticated for her unworldly son.

"Cynthia, you're there. I knew you would be. One can never get him out of his apartment. Listen, dear, I've got it. Just get pregnant. No really, I mean it; it will solve all our problems. You get pregnant, and we'll make a big fuss, and you can move into a bigger place in the city, and he can, oh, go to law school or something." I imagined her waving an elegant ringed hand as she searched for a career for her chronically underemployed son. "I'll pay, of course."

"Sophie, ah, thank you. But I don't think that's what he wants."

"Oh, what he wants. He doesn't know what he wants. He's just slow. Listen, darling, you've got to push him a little."

After I hung up, I surprised myself by bursting into tears.

"Cyndy, don't cry. What's the matter?"

"Your mother wants me to get pregnant."

"I know," he replied. Why hadn't he told me? "She thinks it will make me grow up."

Again that pulse in my brain: why do I stay with him? He's hopeless. It will never work. And I continued to cry because he was sweet and soft and sexy. Because I drove miles every week to see him in his tiny, messy apartment instead of the comfortable townhouse I had worked so hard to buy. Because he worked half-time as an usher in a movie house — inconvenient times that made it hard to get together with him — so that he, instead of Mama, could pay for his rent and food. Because he spent the rest of his time doing absolutely nothing, as far as I could tell, unless I were there to nag him into some activity. Because I was tired of all the effort I put into the relationship and could see no future in it. Because my friends thought I dated him only for his looks and were beginning to doubt my sanity. Because I loved him. Loved him for his very unworldliness, a reprieve from the striving and busyness of my job; for his childlike delight in the world and his confusion as to what to do in it; for his affectionate nature; and for his immense joy in me: a warmer more exciting Mama, who came to bed with him, appreciated him, and made him feel like a man.

"Cynthia, please don't," his voice interrupted my list making. "Why are you crying?"

"I'm afraid we may have to stop seeing each other." It came out before I thought about it.

"Why?" A thin high wounded cry. The fear and pain in his voice surprised and moved me. But how could he be so shocked when I had told him over and over how hard it was for me to come here? When I told him how I needed him to visit me sometimes? Or for us to live together? He hadn't heard me. That's how he survived in his strange, limited world. He didn't absorb the information that would disturb him. And how could he expect me not to be hurt when he never heard me? But he did expect it. For him intentions were all, and toward me he had only the best of intentions.

His hand was stiff in mine. Poor dear. I stroked

it, sorry I had frightened him with the truth. It made me sad. The words "I love you" stuck in my chest. I couldn't say them because he wouldn't say them back. He'd only kiss me and look scared, so they weighed down the air between us, and I preferred that pressure inside me rather than out in the world. But I was too much a mama and too much in love not to console him. "It's just so hard," I said. And then, because he wouldn't understand that, I added, "I guess your mother depressed me."

He squeezed my hand. "Don't talk to her if she makes you upset. I should have said you weren't here."

"No, I like her." I kissed his cheek and knew how much he pleased me and that I must leave him.

Later that day he had a plan. Perhaps his fear had stung him into action. He entered into the project with uncustomary energy. We would release balloons into the wind on the hill above his apartment. He must have gotten the idea from the helium machine in the drugstore where we'd stopped earlier to get me some aspirin. We would attach postcards to the balloons for whoever found them to send back to us, telling us where they had landed. I agreed that it sounded like fun. Anything to lighten the heaviness that had plunked onto my chest, the way my cat did when I lay in bed reading.

We returned to the drug store. I chose a white balloon, milky with a purple squiggle. He chose yellow, which he insisted would be easier to spot. I enjoyed watching the helium slowly pumped into mine. The white turned translucent, then clear, the purple stretching to mauve. His was less attractive; the yellow faint and blotchy, the wan color of illness.

"We have to launch them as soon as possible," he commanded, "before they lose any air."

Back at the apartment I didn't know what to write on the card. He filled his with lies about a junior high school weather project. "They'll be more sympathetic if they think we're kids," he explained. Finally, I just wrote, "Please return to" and his address.

"Why not your address?" he asked.

"Oh well, because this is where they came

from." I didn't tell him it would make me too sad to receive the card one day, when I was no longer seeing him.

He fussed with his postcard, carefully enclosing it in a plastic bag before tying it to the string. Why not put this precise energy into planning a career, I wondered. "Hurry," he urged, "it's getting dark."

I haphazardly wrapped string around my card and tied it on, ignoring his disapproval. The heaviness still held me. He hustled me up the hill. It was pretty at dusk: the houses glowed on the city's slopes. A few west-facing windows flamed orange with the last of the sun, and a faint luminous pink in the east tinged the skyscrapers downtown. "Here, right at the top." He tested the wind. "Face east. You count down."

I did, pausing to breathe between numbers, stretching it out. "Ten...nine...eight...seven (stumbling over the two syllables)...six...five...four...three...two...one (it was over, as inevitable as sunset)...zero." He released his string and the balloon shot into the sky, then seemed to slow and wafted east.

"Why didn't you release yours? You were supposed to release yours." His voice was peevish, genuinely angry.

"Oh. I didn't know. I thought you were going to count down for me."

"They were supposed to go at the same time. You spoiled it."

"I'm sorry. Here, I'll do mine now." I opened my pinched fingers. My balloon took off — up, then east, following his. We watched. His vanished first, but I thought I could see mine glint and circle in the sky for a long time after.

"Wasn't that romantic?" he asked, draping an arm around my shoulders. "But you should have let yours go with mine."

I continued my vigil, imagining a speck of circling light near the horizon.

"It's getting cold." He started down, then noticed my absence. "Hey, aren't you coming?"

"No," I answered. "I'm never coming down."

WOMEN IN JAZZ

The Girl from Ipanema

I lie in bed. This morning I slept with my lover. My lover. I turn the words over with my tongue like lemon candies. Delicious, adult words. I'm eighteen; my childhood breaks off and drops away from me like a coin tossed from the side of a boat. It sinks as I float away from it, lying on my back, looking up, erased of everything but this morning and him. We woke all tangled together in the center of the bed and there was sweat where we touched, my thigh over his thigh, his arm under my neck, the damp sheets clumped around us. Thinking about it, I feel as though a hand has grabbed me in the groin. If groin is the word for that place near the stomach, right above the pubic hair, that place where I feel a pull of pleasure when I think about sex that I don't feel during. During I am marveling. How my legs are open, bent at the knees making a butterfly. How his body is closer to mine than any other body has ever been. How it is I who am making him happy.

He jumped up and went to work. I lie in bed, watching the sun turn milky on the white walls, listening to the liquid chirps of birds gradually still, feeling the air solidify around me, the unavoidable presence of a summer day. I like the day sneaking up on me like this. I remember when I was little and lay on my back in the back seat of the car and watched the tops of trees go by, and the gaps, the sky hazy white and blue. I didn't know where I was going. The car carried me along and it was mysterious too; all I could see of it was the ceiling, domed and padded with a round plastic light in the center.

Now I laze, not sleeping, not waking. My attention moves from the spot of light sliding along the wall to the watery shadows of trees on the ceiling. I don't look out the window where I know the birds have long since left the branches. The birds are a presence signaled only by their sound, which is large and urgent and seems to have little to do with the insignificant brown flutterings I sense sometimes out of the corner of my eye.

My eyes rest on the curve of my shin, which is smooth, tanned an orangey brown, and pleasing. I touch my skin — my thigh, up over the hip to the place in the waist where it tickles — a forbidden place on the side of my stomach that shivers in exquisite revulsion at any touch. So I shift away subtly when my lover's hand is there, but I wouldn't tell him not to, wouldn't tell him anything.

I flex my foot and waking feels so good that I spring up all in one leap. Here are my breasts, small and high on my chest. I am fond of them. I like to look down on them across a smooth stretch of tanned skin. Even when I don't look, I am conscious of them there. I feel others looking. They are a public part of me, the opposite of the private place on my stomach. I feel a little shy about them, but they are outside of my control.

I pull on a shift, no underwear. I stuff my

bathing suit, a towel, a book, some money, and the front door key into my bag. Outside the pavement is luxuriously hot under my bare feet. Mica in the sidewalk shoots sparkles into my eyes. My brown legs flash as I walk. I feel my thighs brushing against each other at the top, feel a trickle of semen, feel my whole body loose and compact and moving under my dress. I own the street, midmorning, summer, so hot that everyone who is not at work — invalids, housewives — is hiding in the house. I think about the housewives, dedicated to their men, wiving the houses for them, their days in precarious balance, tipping toward the moment of homecoming. I imagine them with their blinds pulled down, drinking gin in the bathtub, waiting.

My bare feet make a satisfying slapping sound on the burning pavement. They are so calloused I can walk on almost anything. The sun presses a heavy hand on my shoulder; sweat pools under my breasts and slicks the tendrils of hair hanging in front of my ears. I revel in the heat. It pricks my whole body into consciousness. It challenges me to make it to a spot of shade under a tree at the corner without curling the soles of my feet so I walk only on the hardened edges.

I make it to the tree, step down from the curb. A different texture on the road, rougher, oozing tar, which will stick to my soles for several days until it falls off or wears itself away, I never know which.

I am proud. I am a creature of summer, thriving on the heat. The world shimmers around my body. My body shimmers to meet the waves of heat, of air wrinkled on the edges of things like the quick mirages of puddles on the street, as if sky and earth were blending.

But now the world shifts. I am observed. I am uncomfortable. A woman stands in the flecked shade a tree's leaves cast onto the sidewalk. She is not young. She wears makeup and a large dark hat. How silly to dress up, to cover so much of your body, constricting it. Older people imprison themselves with so much propriety. I will never be like that.

I turn quickly from her eyes on me. I am curious but afraid to look. Does she disapprove of me — my bare feet, my low cut dress, the absence of underwear? Does she look at me and know, shocked, that I have been sleeping with my lover? Shyness tightens my stomach, my thighs press closer together, my feet curl under of their own accord. I look down at them and see the dirt, just a couple of streaks at the top, but the soles, I know, are black with city grime. I feel her judgment and then my own. These are nice little feet — high arched, smooth, elegant. The toenails are pearly with their own natural pink. I don't need to polish my toenails, wear lipstick or a hat.

I reach the corner and my back prickles under her eyes. I turn, safely out of range. I walk quickly now, feeling a wind from the ocean, smelling that salty hot smell in between the houses. At the last block the world opens in front of me. A glare rises off the sand, whitening the sky, and the wind-muted sounds — of children playing, of the surf — rise too and hover in the middle distance. But I am drawn to the horizon, the boat that seems pasted just there, the tension between the appearance of an end and my knowledge that all this is just a beginning; the world rolls onward, warm and blue and specked with small white clouds, and my eyes try to follow it over the sloping edge of the horizon.

The bathhouse is dark and cool. The wet of the concrete shocks my feet, the darkness blinds my eyes. I stand naked in my cubicle, my feet splayed flat on the soothing damp, my eyes adjusting. I shiver pleasurably in the cooler air. I sit and languidly pull on my bathing suit, pausing to inspect a flap of peeling skin on the outside edge of my left little toe. I think again of how it was: he was touching me here and here and here. The weight of his body. How near our bodies were together, a new invention.

I hear voices, shuffling at the door and hurriedly sit up. Now I must make my appearance. I edge past the toddlers milling in the entrance, ignoring the tanned, skinny mothers who attempt to herd them in. The glare rises to slap me in the face. I pause for a second, gathering myself so that I will not vanish when bombarded by the attention of others, their impressions erasing me. In a tiny motion no one can see, I shake myself, arranging my parts. The sun seeps into me, settles on my shoulders. It gives me courage. I look around. People are all occupied with their children, with books or balls, with each other. Their legs touch as ours did last night, but this public touching lacks the intensity of our secret touching, a thing of night, of sweaty summer morning, of the room where the light slides stealthily through the window, toward our bodies mingled on the bed.

No one is paying attention to me. It is safe to start my walk toward the sea. Then I pass the food concession and the man sitting in front of it, his long legs stretched out under a flimsy metal table, is watching me. He was there yesterday, the day before too. He is old, at least forty. I turn away quickly but remember a drooping mustache. And his eyes. It frightened me, yesterday, that stare. I felt crushed by the weight of his attention. I am still a little frightened, enough so that I halt. I am also angry. What right does he have to look at me that way? (He may have a right. I do not know the rules). What obligation do I have toward him? I do not understand the language of attraction, the currency exchanged. If I see his stare, does he

have some power over me, the right to rape me?
Is my lover protection or proof of my availabil-
ity? The old have no right to the young, I think,
but they always act as though they do. As though
my high breasts, my smooth legs made me public
property, gave them some sort of lien on me.

So I am halted, thrown off track by this old man's
stare. I hover between anger and fear. Then another option occurs to me. What would happen
if I responded? If I smiled at him, who would
have the power? I don't know the answer, but
the thought propels me past him. I almost wish I
had the courage to look, gauge his reaction. What
have I signaled to him? If I turned and waved
would he follow me slavishly? Or would he dash
after me, grab me, sling me over his shoulder?

I imagine us together as my feet pad on the hot
sand. He whisks me off to an island. He owns a
boat or an airplane. We are surrounded by sea
at his villa, and all that spaciousness, that ocean
with no continent at its back, makes us feel airy,
lighter, suspended almost.

In this atmosphere I float a few feet above his bed. His face floats over me, the lines standing out in bas-relief a few inches from the surface of his skin. I notice the thick dark hairs in his nostrils. Unseen, his hand drifts over me, parts of me rise to meet it, then sink, as he moves on. The thought floods my groin; a wave of hot liquid spreads through me. No one sees this. All the while I am walking away on the beach like the girl from Ipanema, showing him my swaying back, my hips tight, moving up, down, up, down like the tin limbs of a toy soldier, pulling in, in their effort to escape observation, but telling him this story.

Yes, I feel my body rising to his hand. How each part lives under his touch, quivering, seen. Does this old man look at me in a way my lover cannot? I am seen. I am touched. His eyes tear with the intensity of his attention. I see a fleck of saliva at the corner of his mouth. He drools over me. I am not disgusted by this evidence of his mortality, though I shut my eyes to better feel the lightly traveling hand make my dips and protuberances undulate, a road shimmering in the heat. Is it his awareness of death that makes him see me so, his decay that forces him to surround me, suck me up into himself? My body rises to him. I have left all anchoring. His face is the sun I swim toward. In that heat I will explode. I will have an orgasm. And will I like it?

Something Cool

Thirty-nine, no, forty-two, thirty-seven at the youngest. The oldest? The mirror whispers back fifty. But today is a bad day. The heat flattened my hair; I didn't sleep well. If only I could get a good night's sleep, I'd look younger.

The mirror laughs at me, denying it. The mirror, my enemy. No, we're merely temporarily estranged. These things are my enemies: glaring lights, hot days, daylight itself, young girls.

Young girls. To think it is to hex myself. Here comes one now, pushing past me. A quick confident look in the mirror, a smear of red on her lips, snapping her purse shut, leaving. She didn't even look at me. I'm not worth her attention. Is that really any better than the contemptuous stare of that one on the street today, walking by so brazen in her bare feet. She looked and quickly looked away, dismissing. I am angry at her ease of showing skin. Angry at my own skin that can no longer be shown. Angry at nature, at the years, at the way the world would throw me away.

Back to work. I fight, force the world to accept me. I spread my weapons on the rim of the sink. The pancake shows, but the light is dimmer at the bar. These hot cloudless days the light is so harsh, I have to hide under a large-brimmed hat. My jaw must be firmed. My eyes are large. Purple will do nicely. I had a purple evening dress once; purple satin snug around my breasts, deepening the shadow of my cleavage. I could fall in love remembering. And how the men did fall in love. Fall into that thin cleft. A warm purple starry night, the smell of jasmine in the air. Star jasmine, I put some in my hair. I danced with them all, their lips trembling, their heads held stiff with effort to keep from looking, falling into the jasmine-perfumed purple of my breasts.

That was me. That is not me now. It is a story I tell myself, others too, sometimes when I've had too much to drink. I shouldn't tell it. I shouldn't drink. I should eat at home, stop wearing so much makeup, stop looking for a man in bars.

Thirty-seven, forty-two, fifty. Why bother

looking for a man at fifty? Who would want me? But they did, they always wanted me. I'm not making it up, though I did have a gin and tonic or two. It was real, the way they wanted me. The flowers they sent, the corsages. An orchid is almost indecent in its invitation. My sex sitting there on my shoulder. When they were kissing me they might brush against its pale fleshy petals. It might reach for them, pulling them down.

Why am I such a fool? My skin is flaccid there too. Remember what the mirror says; remember there's supposed to be more to a woman than the mirror, the skin. Why is it so hard to believe that? What do I have besides this face? It is how I know myself. But I don't know myself sometimes when I catch a sideways glance and the haggard stranger standing there scares me. How shallow not to recognize anything else, and not in my interest, either. But I don't. It's like church when I was a child.

They told me about God and I sat still trying not to rustle my starched petticoat, which pushed my dress out deliciously above my thighs, my legs demurely crossed at my ankles encased in my favorite white socks with a rim of frilly lace. I listened and looked and didn't understand. God was a statue with pretty hands and feet pierced by nails. God was the stained glass window, the lollipop reds and greens that paled the light and our faces. God was the organ that made the pew tremble under me. When I left the church, God was gone. I could never find him again until next Sunday, though I tried, imagining with a delightful tremor those languid hands and feet. My first crush. The only unrequited one. How they worshipped me. It made me uncomfortable sometimes. They prayed to me, and I — an oval white face, a cloud of dark hair, a stretch of shining leg between the puff of my dress and the high-heeled shoe which arched my foot so delicately — listened impassively but was secretly perturbed by their entreaties, wondering if that stone statue I so admired as a child had felt similarly helpless.

A dot of rouge. That's better. But still not thirty-seven. Definitely early forties at best. It's the heat. One can't look one's best in this heat. I better remember that when I go out there. No drinks. No childhood stories of Jesus. Not when I'm looking forty. Save that for winter. I'm well preserved in the cold. Damn, my mascara's running already.

If only bathrooms had their own exits, so on a bad day, a day when your makeup wouldn't do its job, when you drank too much and said something you shouldn't, when you needed an escape from the wrong man waiting outside, when the place was full of young girls and you couldn't face it anymore, you could gracefully repair to the powder room and escape.

Who would have thought I'd ever need to escape? I was always so cool, aloof, goddess-like as a statue of white marble. I had my pedestal. My beauty chilled men: put them on ice. They entered my presence as they would enter a moonlit garden: the smell of jasmine in the air, the splash of a fountain, the muted strains of music from the house, the light from the windows gilding the terrace, but not quite reaching me.

I've stepped down from my pedestal now. Even marble would melt in this heat. I'm in ruins and it appears that no amount of restoration will repair me. Marble? Look at that papery dry skin around my eyes. My mascara has run down my face in smudges. I should get out of here. I should have run off with him that time. That time in the hotel room when he begged me and I said no. No because I could imagine begging him to stay one day when I looked forty and the skin under my eyes crumpled like paper. I was sinking down and down on the bed; he was drilling me into the ground, and the ground was falling beneath me. I was sinking through the bed down from the ninth floor, through the lobby, the basement, the earth. I would always need to be filled, would always need him, would always need, this all-enveloping emptiness, this mouth-vagina swallowing emptiness, swallowing everything, this hole.

No, I could not. I could not run away with him. I could not be that. On my knees. I will never get down on my knees. Why am I fooling myself? What is going out there today, every day, if not begging?

Begging for a man. I, who so many have kneeled to, have become the supplicant. I should learn to grow orchids, sip memories, warm my hands over old photographs. Teach my chilled bones to love the heat. No, never. Cracked marble can be beautiful too. Tomorrow will be better. My face is as good as it's going to get. Adjust the dress, the hat, the smile, open the bathroom door.

Walk past the bar. Don't talk to anyone. Don't drink. Well maybe one for the road, something cool.

Since I Fell for You

He probably won't call tonight. I can't expect it. But I do. My stomach twists when I say he won't. An emptiness expands in my chest. I know the symptoms. I will call him soon. But he isn't answering. He wasn't half an hour ago, or last night, or the night before that. And I tell myself that I can't live without his call, can't live through another night of waiting. Though I have, and I will, and more and more the nights are call-less, the stakes are lower, for once it was a night without him that I could not live through, and before that a night when he did not stay till morning.

But I'm alive. My pain tells me. I know I'm obsessed; I know it's hopeless. How did it happen? How did I give myself away? I could have ignored him, that stranger who stared at me. He was nobody then and I was free to turn away, unentered by him, unfettered. I thought his stare was arrogant. I wanted to insult him, to do what an older friend had taught me at twenty — stare back contemptuously, then turn decisively away. But then he smiled at me with such a joy, such a mask of openness, that I was hooked, caught on the jagged corner of his smile. This happened at a restaurant, but I always imagine it on a bus. As though his smile stuck me to my seat, and I didn't get off at my stop and traveled to a new neighborhood entirely.

The phone might ring soon. At some cafe, drinking cappuccino, he might put down his newspaper, take his phone from his pocket, and tell me he's coming tonight. Or he's there at the cafe, but he won't call. He's with someone — the woman in the restaurant, the girl he watches at the beach. Before last night she was my greatest misery. He describes the way her legs move, an eighteen-year-old's legs. Why should I feel old; he's older than I? But I do. I look at my legs and wonder what's wrong with them. I look at all of my body these days, asking what's wrong. Why doesn't he speak of me with admiration? Why doesn't he smile at me? I annoy him now. I know I'm doing it and can't stop myself. I see the muscles tightening around his mouth when I ask for something and know I shouldn't ask; that is what angers him, drives him away. The girl at the beach doesn't ask for anything, doesn't even look at him, and that is so relaxing, like gazing at a stretch of ocean and sky. Then he can turn away. I'm always calling him back, always asking for something. It would be so much better if I didn't. If I were very still, if I turned myself into a mirror, if I never spoke, but only sighed with pleasure, reflecting back his prowess, his power, then would he smile at me?

But I can't. The very absence of his smile prevents it, the knowledge that he's giving it — my smile, the smile I fell in love with — to someone else. To many others.

He'll never forgive me for chasing him down. Before I knew him I would never have forgiven myself. That was in my old neighborhood where life seemed to happen mostly in the day: sun flooding the scene, everything so simple and pure and empty. I walked down a long street; I did the familiar errands, stopped at the familiar locations. I was lighter then, freer, imagining that I had a self, that I had choices, that there were things I wouldn't stoop to.

Now I live in artificial light. The dim glow of restaurants, the small yellow squares from the window that crawl across the sheets at night, the sheen of the reading lamp glazing my pillow. And when he is here, the light turns golden, the whole place buzzes, the air richer, heavier. It eddies around him, pulling me. Always, no matter what I am doing — peeling a tomato, marinating lamb, touching perfume in the hollows of my knees, taking out the garbage — my attention is drawn to him.

But now, more and more, the phone takes his place. I live with the phone, the way I hoped to live with him. I center my life around it, waiting for his call. If he comes, the phone will bring him. But now, as so often, it sits mute. And if it does ring, most times I am cheated. It isn't him. Or it is him and immediately I am disappointed, for I don't want his voice but his presence, and he isn't coming, or he is coming but only for an hour, or, worst of all, he is angry at me. Tonight he will be angry at me.

I knew from the beginning he would be. Walking into our restaurant yesterday, I felt doomed, driven by some overwhelming impulse, yet certain I was making myself unhappy. What did it matter? I was already unhappy. I'm not a fool; I knew that I had already gone too far to recover his love. This act, no matter how dramatic, made no difference. I sat alone near the door and played with the pink napkin folded in a fan shape on the table. He came in with her, his hand on her shoulder. She wasn't the girl at the beach; I could tell right away. She wasn't eighteen; she was my age at least. She had dark hair fluffed around her face. Her features didn't stiffen as mine did; she didn't know about me, didn't notice. He did and glared at me, then turned away determinedly; that was all the acknowledgment he was going to give me. I should have left, but I wobbled to their table. She looked up from arranging her napkin on her lap. Her face was blank, the only emotion curiosity. Could it be that she didn't care about him? His mouth contorted in the effort to conceal his rage.

How I wanted his smile then, the simple pleasure at my presence that had taught me I existed. I drooped, my face crumpling in fear. I squeaked out a greeting; he introduced me as an old friend. His voice was thin with hatred. I knew I would be punished.

He hasn't called all day. Will my punishment be permanent exile? That will come, if not now, later. It is as inevitable and unimaginable as death. I sit here, watching the phone, afraid of its ring, afraid of it not ringing. It rings. I jerk up. "I'm sorry," I say, "I know it was stupid. Since I fell for you, I've been so stupid."

"I've only dated her a couple of times." His voice is calm, almost affectionate; he sounds as if he's telling a story. "I don't really know her. She doesn't seem that interesting. I felt drawn to her because she reminded me of a woman I loved. The only woman I've ever loved." He speaks softly, caressingly even. He tells me the woman he loved was aloof, cool and distant. "I never knew what she was feeling, never knew if she really cared. It kept me interested. I felt insecure with her because I wasn't sure she enjoyed me sexually. It became a challenge. I didn't ask, but I watched her carefully for signs of a response. Then one day I got it. We were in a hotel; we'd been out late; I was exhausted. Still, there was something so provocative about her as she bent to take off her high heels that I decided to try. I lifted her to the edge of the bed, knelt beside it, slid up the skirt of her purple evening gown, and kissed her through the lace of her underpants, feeling with my tongue its roughness slowly dampen." His voice is low, seductive. He's never done that with me. I press my hand between my legs as he speaks, feel the pulsing there. "Finally I pushed the strip of lace aside, and entered her, holding her arms above her head with one hand, while with the other I pulled down the top of her dress, took first one and then the other nipple in my mouth. Her cry when she came was a high whimper; her hands gripping my shoulders tightened and released. Then she got up, told me to leave, and refused to see me again."

He hangs up. And I am left with the phone in my hand, the moisture between my legs, the pain in the center of my chest, more in my lungs than my heart, a suffocating emptiness. "The only woman I've ever loved." I was sure that he had loved me, once, in the beginning. It was all that kept me going: the memory of that love, the memory of his smile, his hands holding my body.

Señor Blues

Well, that's done. What a relief. I don't think she'll bother me again. I may have been a little harsh, but she came looking for me yesterday. And found me. What did she want? What could I do? It's over. As the song says, Señor Blues has gone away.

I stepped into this bar after I phoned her. It's dark, a little cooler here than the hot outdoors, surprisingly full. There are a few women. I can't make out their faces yet. What kind of woman comes to a bar on a summer afternoon? What are they looking for?

What are they all looking for? What can I give them that I have not already given: my admiration, time, attention, my best effort for as long as I can give it?

That isn't enough for them. Depth is not enough; they want length. Not a sixty minute man, a sixty year man. It's not possible, not real. Don't they know what happens in a marriage — how love stretches so thin and brittle it might as well be broken and often is. I don't have that staying power. Some men do, but I could never understand it. How can you allow love to turn so dry and faded, mundane, ugly even? What is sacred about seeing each other picking noses, cutting toenails, nagging, criticizing, snapping about minor irritations, petty differences as though they were the world?

What I offer is something else. I keep love beautiful, exalted. No woman has ever turned to me in ragged underwear, curlers, a bad mood. I make sex a mystery, deep as the blue of evening before it vanishes into night. It is a celebration, a sacrament, the host we can partake of only when we are at our best.

Things change. The world does that. We can't pretend it does not. Why would a woman want me when I don't want her? I don't want to hurt anybody; I just don't understand. Women are beautiful, graceful. Why can't they let go with grace? Why do some hang on so hard I have to push them away? What are they hanging on to?

Not me, a man who never promises faithfulness, only passion. They don't see me; they have invented someone else entirely.

I sip the drink I ordered. It is watery, no longer cold. I'm not often in bars. I prefer brighter places: little cafes with tables on the sidewalk; my favorite restaurant, its large windows all open in this summer heat; the beach, bodies turning in the sun. What a disappointment that a love should end this way. She is a soft thing, with delicate wrists and ankles. Who would have thought she'd be one of the ferocious ones?

The world can be so plain, such a disappointment. It promises so much it doesn't give. When I was young, it was tender. I thought things stayed. How angry I was when I found they didn't, that promises are not kept. I walked around explosive, wanting to punch the air, the absence in it.

I fought with everyone, boys much bigger than me. I came home bloody, bruised, but it didn't do any good; she was not there to comfort me, salve my wounds, see what I had done for her.

That was the hardest — she was not there forever. Not out late, gone overnight, a two week vacation when my grandmother came and I punched her in her soft stomach (I was only four and couldn't do much damage) saying, "You're not my mother. You're not her. Don't kiss me. You're not her."

She was gone. She was not coming back. My head knew it, but my heart played tricks. She'd walk around the corner, her face above some winter coat. I'd wait for her to see me, smile the wide smile she gave only to me, open her arms as though I were little again and would jump into them. But she didn't, and, as she came closer, her face faded, became someone else's, some woman, some stranger I hated.

Then I'd ball my hands into fists, angry at her, the world, myself. I'd think how the last year I'd become too old for her. How I'd squirm away from a kiss, embarrassed, yearning. I wanted it and also wanted to be too big for that. I'd begun to be angry even before she was gone. Now I'd clench inside remembering the times I had rejected her. And part of me would think that was why. I was her only love, the one she smiled for, kissed. I had pushed her away, and now she'd gone too far for me to find her.

I might have gone on like this forever, killed

myself or gotten myself killed, but I discovered
girls. They were my salvation. There were so
many, and each was different, beautiful in her
own way. I was not a snob, unlike most boys that
age. I didn't care only for the popular, recognized
beauties. I admired them all, saw the loveliness of
each. A large girl who was mocked by the others
had perfect lips; I remember the curve of them,
the plump lushness. A studious girl with glasses, uninterested in boys, had long, dark lashes.
There were tears, even back then, when all we did
was kiss on porches. I couldn't understand those
tears, regretted them, but could do nothing to
stop them. Didn't they know the need to experiment, the thrill of someone new? Popular girls
too, who had lots of boys to choose from, why
should they cry over me?

I continued growing up, growing into older
girls, women, sex. The first time I did it — with
a girl two years older than me, her dark wavy
hair with glints of red falling beautifully over her
skin — I knew that this was what I was born for.
So much more of a woman to discover and ex-
plore. And they showed so much more of their
selves, the secret part that stayed hidden under

their prettiness, their soft voices, their elaborate clothes. Nothing then could stop me.

One woman almost did. I was a man by then, not so young anymore, though not old either. She was a beauty, all of her lovely, like my mother. But that wasn't what held me; the world is full of beauties. She was a kindred spirit; I felt her experimenting as I did, holding something back, observing her effect, looking over my shoulder toward her next conquest.

I sensed she didn't enjoy sex with me, and that made me desire her more. Desire for what I couldn't have, one might think, but when I got it, I wanted to elope with her, proposed marriage. A temporary insanity, for how could I be married?

She said no; she left; she broke my heart there in the hotel room with the huge bed, the ornate wall paper. I cried after she left, laid my head on the stiff bedspread and sobbed, tasting my tears. I couldn't go on without her. She wasn't coming back. I knew it. I was used to this loss, expected it. I went on. I never forgot her, but I never tried to contact her, never even tried to find out how she was doing.

It was a relief. Now that I knew a woman I

wanted to stay with wouldn't want me, I didn't have to feel guilty. All women still interested me, but the ones I pursued most avidly were the ones who seemed indifferent. I fell in love with the chase, the moment just before the capture.

So I make the pursuit more difficult, looking for younger women as I grow older. I am back to wooing girls, with the handicap of my age but the advantage of my experience. If I hadn't left the beach to make my call in a quiet place, I'd still be observing a child barely eighteen by the look of her. She walks to the sea each day with an endearing, self-conscious gait. I've seen her stop to examine the dirty sole of a high-arched foot, standing precariously on one leg and bending prettily from the waist. She knows I'm watching. I'll speak to her soon. It will be easy.

It's all too easy now. I can't find a sufficient challenge. I've become bored, and cruel in my boredom, disgusted with devotion, itching to shake this one off, to get on to the next, who proves no more capable of breaking my heart.

Ah, that one walking from the back of the bar — the ladies' room — she has possibilities. Not young, but there's an elegance to the tilt of her hat. An old fashioned touch. Is she trying to hide her age? That would be an interesting vulnerability. She walks unsteadily. Too much to drink? I don't like that; it diminishes the challenge. She leans against the bar to order. The slant of her chin reminds me of someone. Her type always draws me. She has noticed me, smiles. I'll buy her a drink.

CONSPIRATORS

When Clive broke up with Clara, who worries if she is intelligent, he told her that their relationship was only sexual. When he left me, always unhappy with my body, he said I didn't really turn him on. Our common hurt was what brought us together. We felt he'd negated us, body and soul.

We met at a party in my cousin's backyard. Bonnie steered me past her overpoweringly fragrant jasmine vine to a small woman sitting on the shaded bench.

"Celia, my dear, you must cheer Clara up. She's feeling rotten about a man."

"Really?" I stared at the beautiful, flower-like woman. "Me too," I added after Bonnie strode away. My cousin was too close to our family for me to let her know about the failures in my personal life.

"Aren't they fuckers?" Clara's voice was low and slightly guttural.

The obscenity put me at ease. "Christ, yes, and this one you wouldn't believe."

"Mine was worse."

"Don't be so sure."

We compared notes. Clara's story of a blissful beginning, uneasy middle, and final betrayal was familiar, similar to my story, to the stories which many of my friends tell about their one or two disasters. Then she mentioned the name Clive. The dates of our relationships overlapped. We discovered the depths of his treachery.

We became friends. There was an immediate intimacy between us. We could talk endlessly about Clive with a degree of obsession we hid from others. Clara didn't say, annoyance tingeing her voice, "Why don't you just forget him?" She knew the answer.

We did things together to distract ourselves. We discovered that we liked the same movies, the same parks, the same cafes. We spent much of our days together, since we both worked part-time. I taught art classes to small children and their mothers. She was a secretary to a psychologist who once a week good-naturedly tried to seduce her, while she good-naturedly refused. Jerry was remarkably easygoing. She told me that he didn't protest when she pulled the filing cabinet down on herself by opening the two top drawers at the same time, the day after Clive broke up with her. She sat sobbing, surrounded by papers, until her employer returned from a long lunch and helped her straighten up.

Events take on significance later. Once Clara appeared in the doorway of my classroom, her face streaming with tears. The mothers shifted in their low children's chairs.

"Clar," I ran to shield her from them, "are you O.K.?"

"Yes. Get back to work; I'll wait in the hall." She slid her back down the wall and landed sitting, her knees drawn up, as though she were pulling into a shell.

I returned to the classroom and busied myself mixing paint, my back to the mothers. God damn their eyes, I thought, for the first time understanding the phrase. I didn't want our sorrow to be observed.

"Hope your friend feels better," Mrs. Gruber remarked at the end of class as she pushed Johnny out the door.

"I'm sure she'll be all right." Clara huddled in the hall, staring through the passing procession of knees. "Did you notice the figure Johnny drew today?" I continued. "He's really developing fast. The blue painting..." My eyes were drawn to some movement or change. Had Clara left? I didn't see her. Then she was there again, crouching motionless.

Mrs. Gruber coughed delicately. "The blue painting," I responded, "is very, ah, thoughtful, sophisticated."

I watched Mrs. Gruber click down the stairs, her firm hand on Johnny's wrist as he thumped from step to step. "Come in," I called to Clara. "I've got to clean up. What happened?"

"I just needed to see you."

I put my arm over her shoulder, holding my paint-crusted hand away from her mauve flowered blouse. "We clash," I said, fingering my red apron.

"It's a disguise. So people won't know how close we are."

"Conspirators."

She smiled slowly. "Yeah, it's us against Clive and the world."

Another time she lost me for a moment. We were at an art opening I felt obliged to attend. I edged the crowd with Clara, trying to seem absorbed in Billy Sagan's slick, expensive paintings. "So this is how he does it," I gestured at a large canvas of geometric shapes. "This year's colors; it'll go with any room your decorator designs." I glared at the genial drunk in the center of the crowd. He saw me, flopped his hand, and smiled lopsidedly. "Nice work," I shouted.

I turned back to the wall. There were too many people there that I recognized and might have to speak to, and they were dressed too flamboyantly. What had I been thinking of, coming to an opening without jewelry, a hat, or a period costume? I felt conspicuous. I hated the crowd for their successes, for the way they chatted and laughed, the way they slid, plastic wine glass in hand, from one conversation to another. There was Laura Rogers moving toward us like a ship. I knew what our exchange would be like. I would admire her ponderous ceramic necklace, which, of course, she had made herself. She'd ask me what I was doing and I'd answer that I was still teaching kids and finding time for a few drawings. I'd ask her what she was doing: another grant, a new show opening soon, a choice teaching job.

"Celia?" Clara turned slowly, peering through the crowd.

"I'm right here." I put a hand on her shoulder.

"Huh?" She whirled around. "That's funny. I didn't see..."

"Oh Celia, and who is your gorgeous friend?" Laura bore down upon us.

A few days later we sat in a cafe. I played with the sugar in the bowl. I wanted to relate last night's dream: Clive chasing me into a public bathroom, my terror as I waited in the gray stall, knowing he would enter when the other women left, knowing he had a knife in the pocket of his pale blue jacket.

I wanted to hear how Clara would interpret this, what sexual connotations she would catch. I wanted to spill the frightening dream onto the white tablecloth between us, letting her rearrange it into a daylight phrase.

But a man was watching us. I was angry at the

intrusion, angry at his arrogant expression, angry because I was sure it was beautiful Clara who interested him.

"What's wrong?" Clara asked me.

I leaned toward her. "That man's looking at us."

She turned. Her eyes met his. "Are you looking at us?"

He rose. "Yes, you look too good to ignore."

"Well please stop. We want to talk. You're making us uncomfortable."

He slumped back into his chair.

"Clara, that was fantastic. I never know what to say to them." The man gulped his coffee and left. "I just get so flustered."

"It's O.K. Men looking at us has been bothering me lately too." Her shoulders drooped.

I poked the spoon into the sugar. "I wish we were invisible." I looked up. Clara was gone.

"Clar!"

"Celia?" I felt a hand grope for mine.

"Clara, are you there?" The table where our hands were clasped was empty.

People looked in our direction. What would they do to invisible women? I heaved Clara's weight toward the back door. A small strip of grass behind the building. I crumpled, panting.

"Clara, what should we do?"

A gasp or stifled giggle.

I lay back on the grass. I held up my hand and looked through it at an alligator-shaped cloud. My breathing slowed, sank. The sky darkened. I saw the flesh of my solid hand.

Clara sat nearby, her legs crossed tailor-fashion. She looked alert, interested.

"Celia," a smile of greeting, "you're back. What do you think?"

"I don't know. It just happened. I didn't feel anything. It just sort of happened."

"Let's try it again."

I stared at her.

"Come on. Think about something you want to get away from. I know, that dinner party I told you about, the one when Clive talked to that woman photographer all night and I didn't know anybody." Her shoulders sagged; her image wavered. She was gone.

"Clara, come back!"

"It worked." Her voice was exultant. "Come on, Celia, try."

"I don't want to. Please come back."

"In a minute."

I felt scared, lonely. I thought that there had been plenty of times when I would have loved to be invisible. The high school dances, before I knew better and stopped going. Oh God, trying not to stare at Walter Griffin as he sauntered in my direction, but also not looking away in case he did want to ask me to dance.

I started. I couldn't see myself. I reached for Clara's hand.

We went in and out of being invisible. Our lives didn't change much. Lighter and more pliant than most people, we floated in this new element, entering museums and movies for free, watching others unobserved, though it was hard to remember not to talk, and more than once our voices puzzled or scared some passerby.

Before, we had avoided going anywhere near Clive's house, though we were drawn to it, imagining the blue shutters, the brick stairs, the one pine tree in front. Now, invisible, we walked past it often, gorging ourselves on pain and the freedom to feel it. Once, we peered in the kitchen window.

"Wonder if he still keeps a jar of caviar in the fridge," I said.

"And green olives."

"Ugh," I responded. Clara liked to eat bitter things. I loved everything fattening, sweet or salty.

"You know, he keeps the back door key under the third geranium."

"I know." I thought ruefully of Clive's luck; I had never let myself in while Clara was waiting for him in the bedroom with a book.

"Let's go in."

"Clar!"

"Why not? I'm hungry."

The key clicked, scaring me. We entered cautiously. The house reeked of his presence and I wanted him. I also wanted to smash the antique porcelain Fu dog in the hall, to kick the Oriental rugs into a heap, scrawl on the etchings, and, most of all, to batter the shiny, inscrutable suit of armor that stood on the landing of the stairs. His perfection, his horrible self-sufficiency.

"Clara," I whispered. I had gone into the living room without her. I called into the doorway of each room except the bedroom. If I didn't find her soon, I knew I would wait, visible, on Clive's bed for his appearance, probably with a startled woman holding his hand.

"Hi," she answered in the kitchen. "I'm eating." An enormous sandwich, several layers of cheese and meat, bobbed into the air.

A few evenings later we felt restless. There were no movies we wanted to see and Clara's television bored us. The summer air settled on my shoulders. I stretched my arm; it was like moving through soup. "I wonder what he's doing."

"Fucking."

"Yeah, probably."

"We could go see."

"O.K.," I surprised myself by agreeing.

He was alone. He lay among his colored pillows, the sheets crumpled around him. His body was thin, long. He looked vulnerable, yet closed. We stood several feet from the bed, holding hands, trying to be angry. Clara sobbed once and he stirred, an uneasy sleeper.

"Should we go?" I whispered.

"Yes. Oh, he looks so innocent."

I pulled her toward the door. She reached out as we passed him and laid her fingers on his thigh. He sprang up.

We clattered down the stairs and fumbled with the front door lock. In the uproar of our escape, I can't be sure I heard his voice, higher than usual, shouting behind us.

At my apartment we fell into the two fat chairs. Clara finally spoke, "I bet he was really scared."

Her face twisted between a smile and a sob. My mouth twitched and we laughed.

"Oh God, can you imagine? He must be petrified."

"Good."

"Celia," Clara looked at me eagerly, her full-lipped mouth half open, "Let's go back sometime; let's really scare him."

"Yes." My tongue lay in my mouth like a pastel lozenge. Evil had a delicious taste.

For a week we didn't talk about that night. We stayed visible and watched several movies. On Friday we went to a fabric store. The number of customers surprised us until we realized it was lunch hour. I felt uneasy among the crowd. Clara gasped. "Look." She pointed and vanished.

Clive stood by a table, examining a bolt of blue cotton printed with enormous red roses. The blue matched his eyes and, possibly, his living room curtains. In the daylight, I saw he had gotten very tan.

His head turned, and I disappeared, reaching for Clara's hand. We stood still. I was afraid the shoppers would bump into seemingly empty space, more afraid to try to push through them. Clive bought several yards of the fabric and left with the parcel under his arm. The store began to empty; lunch hour was over. "Let's get out of here." I pulled Clara into visibility.

That evening we went to his room. It was sunset, the sky a tender pink-tinged blue. Colors fluoresced in that light — the geraniums by the door, the roses on the new cloth draped over the living room sofa. We climbed the stairs quietly. Clive lay against his pillows, his right hand resting on an open book by his side. He was looking at some treachery, his eyes reflective, inward. He wasn't thinking about us.

Clara gripped his arms. I sat on his legs and unbuttoned his shirt.

His mouth, like an O, floated above us, the screams issuing from the cream colored ceiling, the round moon scaling the window.

GRAVITY

Anne

The tree. She wondered why it was so friendly to her. What luxury to reach up, grasp the branch that hung over the sidewalk at just the height her arms could reach. Swing, feeling gravity pull her — the unaccustomed weight of being in her body — while her muscles strained, hands tight on the rough bark.

Then her hands slipped, too weak to hold on. Her feet fell heavily to the ground. As she landed, her body left her, and once again she was Anne Bloch — a name that never fit her. She was weightless, unconnected — a bodiless ghost.

She stood a minute, quiet in the afterglow of her body's presence, one hand absently patting the trunk of the tree. "That looks like fun." She swung around at the voice behind her. "Can I try it?"

"It's not mine." She moved quickly out of the way of a tall man about her age. She watched as he reached up, tried to hang, but his legs were too long and buckled at the knees as his shoes scraped the concrete. He let go, shook his curly dark hair in a gesture that seemed too boyish for his age. Somehow this gave away his conceit: an unquestioned self-confidence in his height, his expensive suit, the healthy teeth he bared in his grin, his whole potent, magnetic body.

"Well, I guess it *is* yours," he said. "Shall we walk instead?"

She was too startled to say anything but "yes" and stumbled off, not looking to see if he followed. He did, overtaking her with a long stride then adjusting his pace to hers. He leaned back to look up with a satisfied sigh. "All these trees and flowers. What a change. I'm usually slaving away in the sterile cubicles of downtown San Francisco."

She tried to remember how one ought to respond to this type of remark. Ask a question? "Why are you here today?"

"Ah," he expelled a short breath. "A conference. At the Claremont. I should be at a presentation, but nature lured me out." He smiled at her; his teeth were big and very white. "I'm Mark, by the way."

"Mark."

They walked for a while without speaking, Mark humming an indecipherable tune in stops and starts and Anne, remarkably, feeling her body creep back. It considered Mark's body, measuring it: the heft of it, the contrast of his sturdiness with her own insubstantiality. Her body was pleased. She'd never seen it this way before, so cocksure, arrogant. Saying 'yes, this is fine.' As though it had a right to judge.

"What's your name?" Mark asked.

Her body flew off, alarmed.

He saw its fear. It astonished her that a stranger could read her body better than she. He put a hand on her shoulder to reassure her as she gasped out, "Anne."

"Anne... Annie," he repeated. "Well relax, Annie; you don't have to tell me about yourself now. We'll save that for another time."

Then he took her hand and her body flowed

there, contented. She let it continue its dialogue with him. When she stumbled, he pulled her along, laughing. "Careful, Annie. Come back to earth."

"How'd you know?"

"Know what?"

"To tell me to come back."

He laughed. "Well, first you got this kind of glazed look in your eyes and then you tripped." He stopped and swiveled her toward him, holding her shoulders. "You have nice eyes, strange, kind of yellow."

"My mother calls them amber."

"Everyone calls mine brown."

"Like my hair." Her mother always had said it was such a dull color — why don't we dye it, dear? So Anne cut it short, clipping the scissors as close as she dared.

Mark patted the curls on top of her head. "My eyes and your hair match."

They walked again, then he turned to her and asked. "Do you swing on all the trees or just that one?"

"Just that one; it's the right size."

"You're lucky you're short. I'm so tall I think I

might be structurally unsound."

She examined him wondering if he had trouble with his body too, and he straightened, saluting her. But he seemed sturdy: no loose or crooked parts. "No," she said, "you look sound."

"Glad to hear it. Do you think there's a tree that's the right size for me?"

She considered. "Yes."

"Help me find it."

They wandered along the sidewalk from tree to tree. "What about that one?" Mark asked.

"It's in someone's yard."

"That's all right. I'm a lawyer; I can talk my way out of anything."

He bounded onto the big lawn and waved for her. She took a few steps toward him. He jumped, grabbed a branch, swung.

"Hey," he shouted. "You were right; it works."

"Shush," she whispered.

He plunked down, took her hand and pulled her back to the sidewalk. "See," he said, "we made our escape."

He held onto her hand as they walked. When they had circled back to her tree, he said, "Well, here we are." He stared off into the middle distance, his chin raised. Finally, he looked down at her. "Why don't you give me your phone number."

She rummaged in the pocket of her old orange shirt. He held a pen and paper towards her. She was surprised that her hand wrote the right number. "Thanks for the walk, Annie." He patted her shoulder. "I'll be calling you soon."

He loped off and she turned toward home, her body's presence fading with each step.

Her building. Nearly square to the sidewalk, only room for a couple of hydrangea bushes with flowers so improbable she touched them to remind herself they were real. The front door key to struggle with, two flights of beige carpeted stairs, then her own door. Another struggle with another key and she was in her white apartment.

Two days later he called. "Annie, you're there. I was sure I'd have to leave a message and wait for you to call."

"I'm always home."

"Don't you work?"

"Not now."

"Then we complement each other. I'm always working. Let me give you the number. You can call me here."

She copied the number he recited to her. "Well anyway," he continued, "I thought we could get together Thursday. I'll be at another conference. At the Renaissance Hotel downtown. Could you meet me in the lobby at lunchtime? Say about one?"

She did. Her body brought her there. It traveled on the BART train through the crowded plaza where beggars sat with their legs stretched across the stone, and she felt she should have stayed there with them. But her body kept on walking.

It left her in the hotel. The lobby was so opulent: gilt and chandeliers and too many mirrors. Each reflected, under the gold flecks, her pale face. It looked sickly in this setting where everything sparkled or gleamed. She was a little death sitting there with her white face and her long black coat clutched around her skeleton figure. She found a corner behind a potted palm to hide in. She sank into the plush chair hoping Mark would find her. Or hoping he would not. Her body was nowhere around and she had begun to doubt Mark's ability to attract it.

"Oh, there you are." She jumped up and he

took her hand. It tingled and she peered at him, but he was concealed under a large gray coat and dark hat pulled low over his forehead. She wasn't sure if she remembered what he looked like.

"Are you hungry, Annie?"

"No."

"Just drinks, then?"

She realized she was supposed to decide. That made her nervous. But he waited with his head tilted. What should she say, yes or no? She'd said no last time. "Yes."

They sat on a couch near a bar in one corner of the lobby. Her red wine was too bright; it was frightening to drink something that colorful. He talked about being a lawyer for a big construction company. "You aren't working now?" he asked.

She shook her head, shrinking back in her seat.

"You have some savings?"

"Yes," she whispered.

He scrutinized her. "Oh, that's right. I promised I wouldn't make you talk about yourself. What about our trees? Are they doing all right? Did you visit them lately?"

"They have less leaves."

He laughed and reached for her hand across the low table. "We'll just have to keep them company this winter till they grow them back." Then he gazed at her face and squeezed her hand harder. "Annie, will you?" There was urgency in his voice.

"Will I what?"

"You know, Annie. Come up with me. I have a room."

She nodded.

In the elevator he pushed the top button, then quickly punched three more numbers. "It's a code," he explained. "It gets us up to the suites."

They exited on the top floor. He steered her along a soundless corridor padded with pale gray carpet and wallpaper, then produced a plastic tab dotted with holes and stuck it into a box on a door. It opened onto two rooms with fragile looking antiques and an enormous bed. Mark strode to the window. "Let's have the view." He pulled the curtains.

The day was gray, holding back rain. The hues of stone and glass, sky, water, and mountains made a dark mosaic. She turned toward Mark. Pink-faced, shiny, he unknotted his burgundy tie.

He reached for her hand and pulled her toward him. Her body entered her where they touched: first hands, then chests, then legs. He struggled with her clothes, his, and they tumbled onto the bed. Her body pushed against the warmth and pressure of his bulk. He moved on top of her. Her body stayed. She liked having it there feeling the rub of his skin, the rhythm of his motion.

Later there was a grim determination in the way he held her, plunging in. As though he needed her. At that thought her body seeped out of her like a sigh. He didn't seem to notice. He was very self-absorbed as though he were having a dialogue with himself while bouncing stomach down on a trampoline. Finally he finished and fell asleep. Anne propped on her elbow, watching him.

He woke after a while, rolled to the edge of the bed, and looked at the digital clock on the nightstand. "Six o'clock," he said. "I better call my wife and get going." He paused, looked up at her. "Oh Annie. I guess I should have told you before that I was married. Are you all right?" She nodded. "Good, then." He sat and studied her face. "I'm not very experienced at this adultery stuff. Are you sure you're all right?"

"Yes."

He patted her shoulder. "You stay. It's all paid for." He rummaged in his jacket pocket for his phone. "Suzanne, I'll be home in time for dinner for once. In about an hour."

He hummed as he dressed. He winked at her. She thought he knew how a thrill had run through her at the word 'wife.' Her body returned, draped itself over his bent back as he tied his shoes. He's not mine, she told it. No, mine, it answered.

Suzanne

"I'm home," Mark called, and Suzanne felt her jaw tighten in irritation. He'd said he'd be there half an hour ago; now he was too late to help with dinner.

"Suzanne?"

She took the hot garlic bread from the oven and peeled back the foil carefully, holding her hands away from the pungent steam it released. The gesture became a metaphor. She had to hold herself away from Mark these days, from his moodiness, his swings between closeness and distance.

Enough woolgathering, she told herself. It was a phrase of her grandmother's that came to mind whenever she found herself stopped in the middle of a task, musing. She left the bread to cool and stirred the vegetables on the stove top.

"Oof." Mark hugged her from behind and

sauce spilled over the side of the pan. "Be careful."

"Is that the way to greet your long lost husband?" He lifted her hair and nuzzled the back of her neck.

Why was he affectionate now? He'd left in a foul mood this morning, snapping at her when she asked him to put his dishes in the sink.

She dodged out of his arms. "Let me get this on the table."

Mark walked away. Sulking again. If he wanted to be friends, why didn't he stay and help?

They ate in silence. Suzanne fortified within her hurt and anger. Mark concentrating on slicing fiercely at his meat, then setting his knife down precisely on the edge of his plate. Like one of her five-year-olds at school, she thought. Amused, she felt a lightening, a segment of blue sky showing over the walls of her fortress. "Mark?" she said.

He glared at her, his fork held in front of his chest. "What?"

"Nothing." She took another bite. The lamb was undercooked, pale red, vaguely disgusting. I'm sick of this, she thought. She pushed her plate away and rose. Let him clear up for once.

"Aren't you going to finish?" Mark called after her.

"I'm not hungry."

She stood at the living room window looking at her garden. The patio light was on, and she saw she'd left her trowel out there when she was weeding this afternoon. She'd scarcely gotten half of the sourgrass that had sprung up after the rain. She walked to the hall closet and took out the flashlight.

"Where are you going?" Mark asked as she opened the front door.

"The garden."

"Why the garden?"

She stepped down from the patio. She'd started weeding at the bottom when she got home from teaching; she'd start at the top now. She pointed the flashlight at the ground. It made a yellow circle. There. The circle grew smaller and more orange as she knelt. She laid the flashlight on its side and plunged her hand into the small three-lobed leaves of the sourgrass. She felt for the joint were all the stems met, found it, slid her fingers down to the root, grasped, and tugged. She tossed the plant on the patio and picked up the flashlight.

The pile of weeds grew. Sometimes she found a snail and threw it with a strong overhand into the street, listening for the satisfying crack when it hit the pavement. Once she knelt in a patch of lavender, heard the snap of a broken branch, and smelled the pale pungent odor of it crushed. But it was only a sprig, the bush needed pruning anyway. She rolled the flower between her palms and held them to her face. Such an old smell from a living thing: stuffed cloth dolls, her grandmother's underwear drawer, Easter morning.

Her front door opened, spilling light, and Mark stepped out. "Suzanne?" He turned toward the gleam of the flashlight. "Suzanne, what are you doing?"

"Weeding."

"It's dark, come in."

"I'm not done."

"You're nuts. Come on in."

"I said I'm not done yet."

"O.K., have it your way."

She found another patch of sourgrass and pulled. This was what she needed: the calm of the garden, the reward of a task completed, to counter the chaos of Mark's moods. When she looked up again the door was closed. She worked for a long time, lulled by the rhythm of bending, tugging. When she reached the Morales' wall at the north edge, she stood, yawned, realized she was stiff and cold. That was enough for tonight; she had to be rested for her kindergartners tomorrow.

At the patio she swung the flashlight over the garden, picking out the large lumps of lavender, swords of iris leaves, the rock roses, the spikes of linaria, Mexican evening primroses with their pink cups. It was still lush, overgrown, despite her constant pruning. She had an impulse to crawl under a mound of leaves, pull them over her, and sleep there. Ridiculous in the cold San Francisco night. A homesickness hit her: a longing for hot summer nights, the smell of mosquito repellent, the press of humid air against her skin. Native Californians like Mark could never understand why she missed the summer heat of the East Coast. But it would be crisp there now, the leaves turning. She carried the pile of weeds to the composter at the side of the house, picked up her trowel, and opened the front door.

It was dark inside. She cradled the calm within her, not turning on any lights. Walking quietly from room to room. Putting away the trowel and flashlight. Drinking a glass of water. Finally climbing the stairs in the low light that came not from stars and moon but from the streetlamps. Windows glowed green with televisions, all the nighttime power and motion of the city diffused and spread through the sky by fog.

In the bathroom she brushed her teeth with only the nightlight on, then carefully opened the bedroom door. She felt for her nightgown in the dark, folded her clothes over her chair. In bed she rolled onto her back, letting her body gather weight, imagining sleep stretching ahead of her like a long road. A road from her childhood, rising and dipping over small hills, never vanishing abruptly off the edge of the world as streets did here. Fields billowed around it, edged with trees of a true emerald green, far greener than the drab olive of California. The sky darkened; the green intensified. Then lightning, pronged like pitchforks. And the rain, the first sparse drops, fat as frogs. The downpour, soaking through her clothes, delicious. She threw back her head and opened her mouth.

"Suzanne?"

She woke to darkness at first unfamiliar, a disorientation at the placement of her bed, then knew she was in San Francisco.

She felt loss. It had been so long since she'd dreamt of home. Maybe if she fell right back into her dream, she could return.

"Suzanne." Mark nudged her.

"What?"

His hand was pulling at her nightgown, rubbing her breasts. He hadn't even apologized for yelling at her at breakfast. She drew back. "Mark, I have to teach tomorrow. I get up early, remember?" She turned away.

Anne

The phone rang. It was Mark, Anne knew. It had
to be either Mark or her mother and she could tell
the difference by the second ring. She hesitated a
moment, then picked it up. "Annie?"

"Yes."

"It's Mark. How you doing?"

"O.K."

"I could get away today. Will you be home?"

"Yes."

"Great. I'll see you in an hour or two."

It was always like this. It didn't matter. When
he was gone, he vanished completely, nothing to
disturb her white apartment. It was odd that his
coming into her life had been less disruptive than
buying her furniture. She ran her finger along the
edge of the little table. A lump of paint under the
corner. She had missed it. She picked at it, then
stopped; it would leave a hole if she scratched it

off. A hole with the brown of the wood. An expensive wood, mahogany or cherry, she couldn't remember which.

It had been so sudden. First she was at the airport, leaning against a pillar while her mother languidly waved her arm to summon a non-existent porter, though Anne had shown her the cart you could rent by putting in quarters. Then they were whirling through department stores. Her mother patting and prodding the furniture, softly barking orders, spending money. (Had they even stopped home to drop off the luggage? They must have; that's when her mother would have seen the empty apartment.) After her mother left, her place was full of these expensive presences, deep oranges and yellows and browns of wood alive under their glossy varnishes. It was noisy, crowded. Until Anne painted it all white. A good day, a day in her body, stirring cans of thick paint with a flat stick. The big and little paintbrushes with black bristles that curved when she held them against her hand, then stiffened and whitened. The long strokes and short dabs, and carefully wiping around the edges so there would be no dripping, no lumps. But here was one now.

And it was too late to fix it. If she picked it away she'd expose a hole, a patch of color that could spread.

She should be doing something when he came. She took a section of newspaper from the floor, not bothering to check the date, and stationed herself on the couch. She stared at a headline about global warming, then out the window. A tree was trapped between the two apartment buildings; the leaves flapped at her. She tried the article again; concentrate, be studious. When her father came home, she was always reading, perched on the couch in the living room with her books. See, I'm a good girl. He'd walk right past her to his den. Every day she imagined him reaching a hand out to pat her head as she had seen a father do on a television show. But he never did.

Then her mother would hurry through the living room, open the door to the den, not knocking first as Anne was supposed to, and close it behind her. Anne would strain to hear the murmur of their voices. Sometimes she'd go and stand by the door, though she had to be ready to run back to her seat before it opened. She was afraid Mommy would tell Daddy what she'd been telling her all afternoon: that he came home too late, that he took her for granted, that she'd given up everything for him. Her parents would hardly speak to her since she married someone Jewish — and now, look at him, he completely ignored her.

What would happen if they fought? Would they get the divorce that Mommy was always talking about? Would Daddy stop coming home at all?

That hole opening inside her. Scared. Though she was grown-up now, and her father had died when she was thirteen. Still she wanted to close all the curtains, go into the bedroom, lock the door, pull the covers over her head. She couldn't. Mark was coming. She had to sit here on the living room couch, pretend to read, and wait for him. Then suddenly she wanted him to come. She wanted him to talk to her, to tell her she was safe.

She rifled through the paper, looking at Macy's advertisements, the editorials. Calmer. The bell. She stood, heard his footsteps, sat again. Waited for his knock, got up, opened the door. "Annie." His face was large, flushed from running up the stairs, healthy. He put a hand on her shoulder and steered her to the couch. "Sorry, I took so long. My wife called me at work right when I was leaving." He grimaced.

She moved back to the corner of the couch so she could look at him. "Why did you marry someone who isn't Jewish?" she asked.

"Sheer stupidity, baby, that's all."

"Why do Jewish men always do that?"

"You should know. Our mothers."

"My mother isn't Jewish. And she made me get a nose job when I was fifteen."

"Oh. Did your parents get along?"

"My father had a mistress."

"Was she Jewish?"

"I think so. Yes."

"Like us." Mark ruffled her hair. She wondered how he could stand to touch it; it was so dry and brittle. "Is your Mom pretty?"

"Much prettier than me."

"You're O.K. That's why I like you; you're not the standard issue shiksa."

"So you think I'm Jewish?"

"You sure are."

"But why? What does it mean?"

"Nothing."

"It can't mean nothing. My mother's parents wouldn't even come to the wedding."

"So there are bigots in the world, Annie. To hell with them. Try having a name like Shapiro and my nose and hair. You'll really get shit from some people then. I don't let it get me down. Some people are gonna hate you no matter what, and some people are gonna like me just the way I am. Like you, eh Annie?"

She didn't answer him. He didn't need an answer. She looked at his nose. It seemed the right size for his face. It seemed to fit, like hers had when she was young. But her mother had hated it. She felt angry at her mother now. She remembered her discussing her nose with the doctor, while Anne sat there saying nothing. She imagined herself at fifteen speaking up, "Some people are gonna like me just the way I am." Her mother would have stopped talking, stared at Anne with a look of pained surprise. If Daddy had been alive, he would have helped her, saved her nose from her mother and the doctor.

"Off in the ozone again, Annie." Mark pulled

her up from the couch and walked her into the bedroom.

It seemed ludicrous, the ritual of him undressing her while she stood still as she had for her mother when she fussed her into a frilly dress. "You're so quiet, Annie," he stroked her shoulder and her body noticed. "Really quiet. Not just pretending to be but having all sorts of things to say underneath like other women. I like that. How did you get that way?"

"I'm not all here."

He laughed and tipped her back onto the bed. "We'll see what we can do about that."

"It doesn't matter."

"Uh-huh." But he wasn't paying attention. He was sliding out of his clothes. Feeling her body there, squashed under his, even the tug of his hand on her hair on the pillow, was good. She felt heavy, delightedly sunken in her flesh. It lulled her, a jump rope rhythm running through her head: *'Dagwood, Blondie went downtown, Blondie bought an evening gown, Cookie bought a pair of shoes, and Dagwood bought the evening news.'* The words faded into images: a rope slicing through a blue sky, white clouds. She couldn't see the girls swinging it at each end; no one was jumping. It was as though her body itself were the rope circling down, up through the bright sharp air. Then something happened. Her body clenched, released, lifting her. The jump rope floated up, glinted in the sun, grew colors, became a box kite drifting higher and higher, and she was floating there with it.

"Annie, Annie," Mark's hand on her shoulder, his voice tugging her down. "Annie, you came, didn't you?"

"Yes."

"Annie." His arms tightened around her.

It was gone. The floating, the kite, the warmth inside her, the old, old feeling of a paradise regained. But her body was there. Could it do it again? It arched toward him. He slowed after a while and it pushed against him, urging him on. Don't stop. Her body ravenous, gulping at him. Then clamping down on him, no kite this time, just a ferocious stiffening and then satiety, a drifting, sleep.

Waking. She looked at him lying there, his long back curved away from her, covered with dark freckles and a few stray black hairs. He was so big and yet helpless, inert, like a chunk of meat. Her body could swallow him whole.

The next time it was raining. They had finished and lay on the bed. Mark pulled the covers over her shoulders, and Anne half dreamed of her father wrapping a blanket around her and carrying her from the car to the house through the rain. "Oohh," Mark stretched, "I hate to go out in this. I'd rather stay here with you."

"Don't get home too late."

"Why not, baby? She doesn't care."

"She'll think you take her for granted."

Mark laughed. "Don't worry, Annie, when it comes to taking people for granted, Suzanne wrote the book." He rolled toward her and stroked her hair. "Maybe I should get a divorce. I wouldn't have to jump up and leave you all the time."

Anne sat, clutching the blankets to her neck. "A divorce?"

"Yeah, I've been kind of thinking about it."

"No!" Anne flung the covers off and jumped up.

"Annie, calm down." He came over and held

her shoulders. "Come back to bed."

She shouldn't let him touch her, but her body leaned against him. It was still hungry. He steered her to the bed and pulled the blanket over her. "That's better. What's wrong?"

"I shouldn't have."

"No, Annie, don't feel guilty. It really has nothing to do with you. We just don't get along." He kissed her forehead and her body softened. "Feel better?" he asked. She nodded. "I should go now. I'll call you tomorrow." He patted her head, then reached for his clothes.

She heard her door click shut. She had to stop him. Daddy had never talked about divorce; it always had been her mother. Her body had caused all this trouble; she couldn't trust it. Get it away from him. She felt in her closet for her raincoat and rushed down the stairs.

Outside the rain was cold. It wet her hair and trickled down the back of her neck. The sidewalk chilled the soles of her feet. She ran but her body stayed with her. She couldn't shake it. The tree, she'd give it back to the tree. Her feet splashed through a puddle. She raced across the street as a car veered around the corner. On the next block the tree stood in a circle of lamplight. She touched the wet, shiny bark. Her body wanted to hug it. She opened her raincoat and wrapped it around the trunk. Next to her skin the tree felt scratchy and cold, but sturdy, comforting. She leaned her forehead against it and closed her eyes. It was as though she held onto Daddy; she rubbed against him, feeling a warm center in the cold; he was carrying her safely through the rain.

But he hadn't carried her. She remembered now. He'd said it was her own fault for refusing to wear her rubbers; it was only a few steps to the house; it wouldn't kill her to get her feet wet.

They were wet now. Her body was gone. She buttoned her raincoat and walked back to the house.

Suzanne

Suzanne had a book propped against a canister behind her plate. Mark was sleeping in; she'd waited and finally started Saturday breakfast without him. Or was he taking one of his long showers? She listened but couldn't hear if the water upstairs was running. She sipped her tea and turned a page. She hoped they would go somewhere today — a hike maybe, get out of the city. She was trying to be patient.

Mark padded into the kitchen, tying the sash of his maroon bathrobe. His wet hair was slicked back though the curls would spring up as it dried.

"There's pancake batter," she told him.

"Thanks." He sat down. Waiting for her to cook it for him. Myra had pampered him so thoroughly that even now, after fourteen years of marriage, he automatically expected a woman to provide for his every need. If brides got to know their future mother-in-laws' habits, Suzanne thought wryly, a lot of weddings would be called off.

"Suzanne?"

"Yes?"

"I've been thinking about that Hoffman project; I really have to go in today."

"All right." No point in even mentioning the hike. If he didn't care enough to save Saturday for her, she wasn't going to force him to.

"You aren't mad, are you?"

"No." She looked for her place in her book.

"I'll be home in time for dinner."

"All right." She tried to concentrate on reading while he made his pancakes, ate them quickly, and headed upstairs to change.

After he left, she slowly cleared the kitchen, her movements languid. Maybe she was too tired to go on a hike. She didn't even feel like gardening. She brought her novel into the living room. She'd just stretch out on the couch and read. Today would be a day off from taking care of people, Mark and the kindergartners.

She sank into the world of her book. When she finished it, she gazed out the window; at first unseeing, then noticing the late afternoon sheen of the sky. Had she spent the whole day on the couch? Her shoulders were stiff from sitting in one position. She felt uncomfortably sluggish as though she were sick and had lazed around all day to recover. She stretched, slowly swung one leg, then the other over the edge of the couch and pulled herself up. She should start dinner.

The kitchen brought back her usual energy. Game hens, she decided, wanting to cook something elaborate to make up for the lassitude of her day. She found them in the back of the freezer and defrosted them in the microwave. And fancy stuffing, the one with the dates. The laborious task of pitting was a penance. She worked steadily, pitting, then chopping the dates, celery, scallions. She liked the rhythm the knife made on the board, the swift, sure movement of her hand and wrist. We take pleasure in our competencies, she thought. Maybe that was why Mark spent so much time at work; he certainly had no aptitude for anything at home.

She better call and find out when he'd be back before she put the hens in the oven. She wiped her hands and went to get the phone. His cell was off and no one answered at the office. It would be hard to get through on a Saturday with Adele, the receptionist, off. She'd just have to wait till he arrived.

She mixed the apricot glaze. At a quarter to seven she tried to call again. No answer. She had to start the hens or they wouldn't eat till midnight. Why wasn't he home yet? Why hadn't he called to say he'd be late? She paced around the kitchen with the scrub sponge rubbing grease spots off the refrigerator, the stove; there were even some on the wall above the table. She wondered how they got there, why she hadn't noticed them before.

The timer rang and she took out the game hens. A lot his promises meant. Should she call someone to eat with her? Karen and Doug. No, there wouldn't be enough. Someone single, like Linda? She tried but Linda didn't answer her phone, and she still couldn't reach Mark. She pulled off a leg to nibble and wrapped the rest in foil.

She scoured the dirty roasting pan, her hands soothed by the hot water. Of course he's all right, she reassured herself; he just lost track of time.

But he should have called or at least turned on his cell. He knew it was hard for her to get through after hours. Didn't he realize she'd worry?

She stretched back on her heel to loosen a tight muscle in her calf, dried the pan, and bent to put it away in the cabinet. The motion caught on a memory. Babysitting her brother and sister. Kenny and Carol were hiding, mad at her for enforcing some rule. She couldn't remember what, only the quiet of the house, which felt empty, and her rising panic as she called, then searched, while trying to look calm in case they could see her. Checking everywhere, even in the cabinets under the sink, where they could hardly fit.

What happened in the end that night? Did they pop out of some clever hiding place, gloating, challenging her authority? Or did she search them down, the stern big sister, keeper of her parents' rules?

"Damn him," she said aloud. Though whether she meant Mark, or her brother Kenny as a child, or just the generic male, she didn't know. "I'm going to bed." She marched up the stairs and was brushing her teeth when the phone rang.

She hurried to her desk to answer it. "Hello?"

"Suzanne, hi, it's Linda."

"Oh, hi, Linda." Disappointment, then annoyance at Mark.

"I was returning your call. I just have a second, Gilbert's here."

Gilbert? Oh, that new guy she was dating.

"So what's up?"

"I just called to see if you wanted to come to dinner. I made game hens."

"Too bad I missed it; it was probably a lot better than the stuff at the trendy place we ate at. I hope Mark was properly appreciative."

"He's working late at the office."

"Turd. And he missed your masterpiece. Why do we put up with them? If someone could build a better dildo..."

Suzanne laughed. "So how are things going with this one?"

"Oh, I don't know, girl," Linda lowered her voice. "If he says one more thing about the Forty-Niners, I think I might scream. Don't they know when they're being boring? You'd think when your date takes a twenty minute nap at dinner, you might wonder."

"Maybe he thought you'd swooned in admiration of his insightful analysis."

"Yeah, sure. Oh, I hear him pacing in the hall. I better go."

"Bye."

"Bye. I'll call you Monday with the full report."

Suzanne put down the phone, smiling at the excitement in Linda's voice despite her sarcastic tone. She envied her adventures. The beginning of a relationship — dating, discovering sex with each other, that sense of possibility. What good had the security of marriage done her today? Here it was Saturday night and she was alone. She might as well be single. Then, at least, she'd have a chance of a romantic weekend. She pulled on her night gown and turned off the light. She wouldn't wait up for him.

A hand on her shoulder. Mark. She lifted her head. He was her father walking out of her room from childhood. In the kitchen her mother scolded her, "You're late; they've all left already; you'll miss the bus."

She stood in front of the closet and pushed through the clothes. Carol had left her stuff on Suzanne's side again; it was a mess. She couldn't find anything. I'm tired of being the oldest, she thought. She was really late now. She pulled on a purple sweater set. No, it looked terrible. Then a shirtwaist printed with pink flowers. Too small, she couldn't get it on.

Then she was in the corridor of her high school, late for a chemistry test. But she hadn't studied, hadn't opened the book all year because she was a grown up now; she had a master's degree. Mr. Donovan handed her the test sheet. She'd fail. She wouldn't make the honor roll.

Mark took her hand in the high school parking lot. "Don't worry. I'll drive you home." He kissed her. He was Jimmy Macky, the handsomest boy in school, who'd been her boyfriend for six months in junior year.

Mark drove away in his BMW. "Wait!" She ran after him, but her sandal came unstrapped; she stumbled and fell on her knee. The car receded down a mountain road, appearing and disappearing around the bends, getting smaller and smaller.

A door banged downstairs. The dream dissolved. "Mark?" she called.

After a while she heard his footsteps on the stairs, then he opened the door and stood in the doorway. "Why didn't you call?" she asked.

"Call?"

"You said you'd be home for dinner."

"Oh, I forgot."

"I cooked something special. I was worried."

He stood with his hand on the doorknob. "I'm sorry, Suzanne. I worked late; I'm exhausted. I didn't even have time to think about eating."

"You could have called at least."

"I said I'm sorry. What more do you want?"

"I want you to use your brain next time. You know perfectly well it's impossible for me to get through when Adele's not there. Turn on your cell phone."

"Look Suzanne, I'm too tired to fight with you now. I'll go sleep in the study."

She heard him rustling in the hall closet, pulling down the spare bed blankets, making as much noise as possible. Now he'd probably sulk all Sunday. She felt an urge to get up, go to him, see if they could salvage what was left of the weekend. No, why should she always be the one? If he wanted to pout in the study, let him.

Anne

A disaster. Mark came with roses. A huge bunch; their fat red heads poking over the white paper, knocking together. "For you," he thrust them at her.

"Why?"

"Because you're my girl. Come on, take them. They probably should go right into water."

"What about your wife?"

"Don't be silly, Annie." He pushed them into her hand.

"No. I can't. Give them to her." She shoved the bundle back at him. It bounced off his chest.

Mark stooped to pick it up. "Calm down. There's nothing to worry about. Let me get these in water."

She heard him banging cabinets in the kitchen, muttering, "Doesn't she have any God damn vases?" He returned with the flowers stuffed into a tall glass and put them down on the little table, then sat next to her on the couch.

"Annie, listen." She cringed as he patted her shoulder. "You don't have to throw this fit. You women always think you have to stick together. But it just isn't working with Suzanne."

"No." His hand was still on her shoulder. Her body frightened her — the way it welcomed his touch.

"Yes, Annie. It's true."

"Why?"

"Because she's always right. Because she's so God damn sure of herself, and how good she is working with those kids, and her fucking perfect garden, and her perfect little shiksa nose, and her blond hair, and her perfect skin. Except, let me tell you, that skin is getting dry and starting to wrinkle. She'll look older than me soon."

"It isn't working because her skin is dry?"

Mark threw back his head and laughed. "Oh Annie. Her skin is fine. It's just not easy living with Miss Perfection. Especially when she knows it."

"She's perfect?"

He ruffled her hair. "No more perfect than

you." He paused, letting his hand drop to the couch. "You let yourself be. You let me be. You don't go around judging everyone for not living up to some impossible set of standards. Even when she doesn't say anything, I know. I can see it in the slant of her chin." He stretched back his arms, then reached to stroke her cheek. "Enough of this kvetching. Come on, baby, let's be bad together."

No. She shouldn't. But her body let him pull her up from the couch, lead her to the bedroom.

She lay in bed after he left. I've been bad, she thought. And felt a stirring, another demand. It pushed at her, nudging her out of the bed which seemed so white and comfortable. It led her to the refrigerator, but there was nothing it wanted there. Then the cabinet. Cans of soup, boxes of crackers. No. The sugar bowl. She took it down and stuck a spoon through the hard crust which had formed because she didn't use it. She had never liked sweets. But now she swallowed spoonful after spoonful, shoving the spoon she'd eaten with back into the bowl. She ate it all, then sat in the corner, staring out at the trapped tree. Maybe there was some Halloween candy from last year. She always bought it in case children came, though they never did to the third floor. She rummaged in the cabinet, then climbed on a stool and groped around in the back of the top shelf. She felt a crinkly bag with little lumps inside. She pulled it out, tore the cellophane with her teeth, pushed handfuls of the stale smelling stuff into her mouth.

She stood on the stool with the torn wrapper in her hand, then stepped down slowly and walked to the full-length mirror. She was naked. She had never put her clothes back on after Mark left and was walking around the apartment with all the curtains open. She studied herself — sallow skin and sharp bones, tufts of dry hair. Hardly room for her body there. But it was making her do things.

She couldn't tolerate living with a body that did things without her consent. Why was it sticking around? It had never stayed this long before. She had thought she wanted it but didn't know how to make it stay. Now she couldn't get rid of it. She pulled the spread from the bed and hung it over the mirror. It flopped to the floor and her body leered at her. She picked up the spread and tucked an edge behind the frame. She took a sheet to wrap around her body and climbed into bed. Safe with the sheet pulled over her face. In a white cave like the ones she had made when she was a girl. A good girl. She'd tried so hard. So they would be safe. So Daddy would notice her. So Mommy and Daddy wouldn't get divorced. But Daddy died. And she wasn't safe. They'd told her she had everything, but she wasn't safe. She'd never asked for anything, just taken what was given to her — toys, fancy dresses, the nose job, the furniture, her mother's money that came in an envelope every month. But her body was asking now. How had she encouraged it? By giving it sex? By giving it sweets? She'd have to starve it out.

She curled up under the sheet and closed her eyes. Walking down a road. A long road in flat country, evening, no stars yet or moon. It would always be evening. She would walk forever in the dull light. Stubble of dead weeds on dry dirt. She had to find something growing — the flower that opens in moonlight. She tried to run into the night, but her feet were stuck. Ahead porches with swings, dark windows, houses locked in silence. A streetlight at the start of a dark country road. Night, arriving at night; the flower would open — tropical, lush. She stepped into the yellow cone of light. Something behind her. She half turned. Her shadow. Another shadow rearing over it. She spun around. No one. Still the shadow loomed, knife in hand, and struck her shadow to the heart.

"Daddy," she woke up calling and sat straight up in bed. She shook her head, driving out the dream. But she felt it flitting around her. She turned quickly. It was gone, then there again just out of range in the corner of her eye.

Someone should help her. Mark. He'd told her to call him, but she hadn't. She pulled on her clothes and found the telephone. The scrap of paper with his number was in her top drawer.

"Dryer, Incorporated." A woman's voice startled Anne.

"I need Mark."

"Mr. Shapiro? I'll try that extension. Who's calling, please?"

"It's Anne."

"Annie," Mark's voice came on, "what's up?"

"I had a bad dream. After you left. Can you

come back?"

He hesitated, then answered, "O.K., but not for a while; I have a lot of work to finish."

After she got off the phone, she sat on the couch for a long time hugging herself. She had to be very careful. Daddy had told her to be careful not to hurt her mother's feelings. It was the time she'd dirtied her good dress, playing on the swings in the park before a wedding. Mommy had been busy talking to a friend and hadn't seen her slip away. It had been so terrible when she cried — her face red, her make-up streaking down her cheeks in colored lines — that Anne had run to her father and tugged at his hand, pulling him away from the group of men. He had bent down to her with a puzzled look. Stayed, to her surprise, to listen to her as she tried to talk quickly between her gulping sobs. And told her to be careful.

Having instructions had comforted her. If she were careful, Mommy would be all right. They would be safe. She wanted Daddy to give her instructions now.

She had to hide from her body, to sit very still until he came. As soon as she thought that, her foot tingled. It hurt. She wanted to shake it, stamp it on the floor. No, that's how her body would get in. She tightened her stomach and chest so her breath wouldn't move them. Finally, a knock on the door.

"Daddy." No, it was Mark. "You came."

"I told you I would." He wrapped an arm behind her shoulders. She struggled against her body but it entered her, leaned into him, relishing the warmth. "So, you wanna tell me about this dream?" he asked.

"No."

"All right, what about dinner, then? Would that cheer you up? I'm starving."

In the restaurant she realized that she shouldn't have come. She didn't want to encourage her body. "I better not eat anything," she told Mark.

"Why not? You're thin. Come on, what'll you have?"

"Just salad."

But when the waitress brought it, it was gone in a few bites. She watched Mark carefully cut his chicken half into pieces. Drops of juice formed where the knife pierced the yellow skin.

It smelled good. "Can I have some?"

"Sure." He put a piece on her salad dish. "Hey, I'm not going to let you starve, Annie; I'll order some more. You want chicken?"

"I don't know."

He called for the menu, and she examined it. She wanted something with lots of blood. "A rare steak," she decided.

It lay on her plate. She sawed at it with her knife, finally tore off a piece and brought it to her mouth. It was delicious. It tasted as red as it looked. She took a bite of chicken breast. Yes, that tasted white. She wanted the red; she didn't care that colors were dangerous.

She ate every piece, letting the blood slide down her throat.

Her stomach felt heavy when she climbed the stairs to her apartment. "Did I eat too much?" she asked Mark.

"Not at all. Glad to see you have an appetite." He leaned over and kissed her forehead, then stroked her neck. Her body wriggled toward him. It unbuttoned his shirt and unzipped his pants. Her clothes came off too, Mark and her body working together. It dragged him on top of her.

He was too tall for the couch. Her body scratched at his back, made noises, gulped him down and rose above the couch. The light yellow in the air, a line of blood on his shoulder.

"God, that was great, Annie." He kissed her hair. "Come on, honey, let's go to bed."

"Don't you have to go home?"

"Nah, she won't miss me. Besides, I have to protect you from those scary dreams." He took her hand and pulled her up and into the bedroom, then folded down the covers and flopped onto the bed. "Come on, jump in."

Yes, she needed him to help her. She stretched out next to him, holding his long back, feeling the sweat between their skins. His rib cage moved up and down. He was asleep. She was sleepy too. She felt warm, safe, as she had when she'd peeked into the bedroom and seen her mother and father lying in their bed together. She'd thought they couldn't get divorced if they slept together that way. Mark rolled onto his back, weighing down her arm. He was too heavy. She tried to slide out from under him. Stuck. A trap. Her body had tricked her again.

She pushed against him, and he shifted away

from her, mumbling. She slipped out of bed before her body could catch her and walked to the living room, cradling the freed arm in the other. He shouldn't be sleeping here; Suzanne was his wife. He should be with her. She picked an orange rag up off the floor — her blouse. How did this happen? How did he get her to take off her clothes every time? She threw her shirt across the room at his flowers, but it landed a few feet away. She strode over, dashed the vase to the floor. It didn't break, just rolled on the carpet, spilling water. She picked it up and hurled it at the wall. It shattered, the roses tumbling. A pool of water soaked into the rug. It made her think of the lump of paint under the little table. She found it, scratched, and it came off on her fingernail. There. She'd let the color out. Pouring from the hole in the white paint like water. To drown him.

Why are you mad at him? What? Her body talking.

"Who?"

You've got the wrong one.

"Don't talk to me." She slumped on the floor and put her fingers in her ears.

That won't work: I'm inside you. You have to listen.

You've got to kill him.

"Kill Mark?"

Not Mark, the first one.

Daddy? She couldn't kill him; he was dead. But her body pulled her to that green hillside, Forest Lawn Cemetery. The heaped earth was light brown and sweet-smelling, moist. Dig. They scrabbled in the dirt. Her body down on its knees, soil flying from its scooping hands. She saw the shiny brown casket that had looked too small. *Out,* her body commanded. The casket tipped till it was standing upright. Its top swung open. Her body reached in, yanked the skeleton by the back of the neck, rattling its long bones, shaking its dry skull. Anne stared at it, willing it to look back, to see her with her cut off nose. "You're bad," she told it. "You left us".

Suzanne

The turkey was in the oven. The house was clean. The table set with the good dishes and crystal, and a bouquet of rosemary, mums, and holly branches stood in the center. Suzanne was particularly proud of it, though the rosemary shed green spikes onto the tablecloth.

She straightened a fork, rubbed a water spot on a glass with the edge of her apron, and decided the table was ready. What time was it? Three hours later in the East. She'd better call her family now, before her guests arrived.

A young voice answered the phone. "Aunt Suzanne! Everyone's here. Mommy, Grandma, it's Aunt Suzanne."

Janey, Carol's oldest. She sounded so grown-up. What was she now, eight?

"Suzanne," it was her mother. "Happy Thanksgiving. How are you out there? How's Mark?"

Hearing her mother's soft worn voice speaking of the weather and the grandchildren, Suzanne could imagine the cold gray sky, the dusting of snow on the surfaces, the holiday quiet of the neighborhood, and the contrasting warmth and bustle of the house, filled with the voices of small children and the smells of a family feast. She felt a longing to be there. To preside over the kitchen, to hold Carol's new baby, and most of all to fold her mother in her arms, startling her out of her familiar chatter into a connection they could never make on the phone.

"So I'll give you to Carol... Suzanne? I'll say goodbye now. Here's Carol."

"Goodbye Mom, happy holiday."

"Hi Suz... oh, excuse me, Deidre's fussing. I'll be right back."

Suzanne waited, wondering as usual why Carol and Don had chosen that ornate name for their youngest, so unlike any others in the family..

"Here I am. She was hungry. What a greedy little girl. Can you hear her slurping?"

"I don't know. Kind of. How are you doing? Is she sleeping better?"

"Only up twice last night, thank God. I can see

why Mom was so tired by the time I came along."

"It's hardest when they're infants."

"And this one's the last. You know, Suz, it's kind of funny. I always thought you'd be the one to have a big family. God knows you were like a second mother to us."

"Oh well."

"Are you going to?"

"Well, Mark..."

"Don't let him wait too long. Mine need some cousins."

"I'll see what I can do. Take care of yourself now. Let Don change a few diapers."

"I will. I love you, Suz."

Suzanne paused, surprised by the declaration; her family usually didn't say such things out loud. "Me too."

"I'll get Ken. Hey Kenny, you want to talk to Suzanne?... He's in the middle of football. He says hi."

"All right. I better get off soon, anyway; people are coming."

"Have fun. Maybe next year? Tear Mark away from work and come East for a few days."

"Sure, maybe next year. Give everyone a hug

for me."

"Bye, Suz."

"Bye."

She stood by the phone a minute, her arms wrapped around her chest. The doorbell. No time for woolgathering. She released her arms and started downstairs.

Soon she was in the midst of the party, orchestrating everyone's activities. Doug and Karen were warming up yams in the kitchen. Mark's mother had fussed over which bowl would best display her cranberry sauce. She was now ensconced for a while, Suzanne hoped, in the living room pointing out the features of the view to his elderly great aunt from southern California.

"Should I toss the salad now?" Maria, her aide at school, asked her. Suzanne had invited her because she'd be leaving soon to go back to college and she realized she'd miss her.

"Wait a few minutes. Thanks."

Linda and her date weren't here yet, but that didn't matter. They were bringing the dessert. If worst came to worst, she could start without them. The timer rang. Mark should take the turkey out and sharpen the knives. Where was he?

Not in the living room. "Myra, have you seen Mark?" she asked his mother.

"He hardly said hello to us," Mrs. Shapiro shook her head mournfully, "and he hasn't seen his Aunt Nelda in years."

"Well, I better find him to help with the carving." Suzanne backed out of the room quickly. She was pretty sure he wouldn't be in the kitchen but checked anyway.

"Nah, haven't seen him, probably upstairs watching football," Doug told her. "Hey, come back," he put an arm around her waist and pulled her toward him, "Karen and I have something to tell you."

"What?" Suzanne stepped out of his reach.

"You tell."

"No, you do."

Karen blushed. "I'm pregnant," she announced shyly.

Oh no, Suzanne thought, then ran to hug her old friend. "That's great! Should we tell the others?"

"No, it's too early. We just wanted you to know," Karen answered.

"Well, congratulations. I'll go dig up Mark now, or we'll never eat."

She climbed the stairs slowly, the pressure of tears behind her eyes, and found Mark in the study, watching T.V. as Doug had predicted. "I thought you were going to help me."

"I spent the whole morning chopping vegetables for your stuffing."

"You're not going to eat any?"

"Of course I'm going to eat it. What does that have to do with anything?"

"Well, don't call it my stuffing then."

"O.K. Suzanne, I'm sure our stuffing will be delicious." He switched off the television. "Let's go down and eat it. I was just hiding from my mother and Aunt Nelda."

"Leaving me to deal with them?"

"Come on, Suzanne, I didn't ask you to invite them."

"They're family, and, if I didn't, would you be the one to get on the phone tomorrow when she asks if we had a good holiday?"

"Don't spoil my appetite, O.K.?" He ran down the stairs.

Handing plates around the table, Suzanne

thought the smells were almost right. The only thing missing from her childhood were the radiators clanging and hissing in the background.

People ate, talked, the hum of conversation full and warm. Only Mark sulked, making a chilly spot at his end of the table. It didn't help that he sat next to the two empty chairs for Linda and her date — what was his name, Brian, Robert? She couldn't keep track. She rose and went to sit near him, laying a hand on his arm. "Did you know Maria was going back to school soon?" She smiled at the young woman on his other side.

Mark held his silence for a moment, then gave the girl his usual charming grin. "Oh really? In what?"

"Well, first I have to finish the prerequisites, but then I want to study psychology," Maria began in her breathless, quick-speaking voice. Suzanne detoured through the kitchen to refill the water pitcher, then settled into her seat.

The doorbell rang. Linda burst in. "I'm sorry I'm late. Here's the pies. Where should I put them?"

"The kitchen."

Suzanne followed her long stride. "Let me

find room for them in the fridge. Where's..."

"Gilbert. We broke up." Linda pushed back a strand of her dark hair that had escaped from her barrette. "Let's get to the table; I'm famished. I'll tell you about it later."

She swiveled into the chair next to Mark. "Better late than never," she announced to the group. "I'm Linda. I think I don't know a couple of you."

Suzanne made introductions, then relaxed. She'd let Linda take over for a while. She could trust her not to ruin a dinner party no matter what was happening in her personal life. She had a lawyer's unshakable poise. Like Mark, Suzanne thought, watching him speak more loudly, gesture more expansively, responding to the competition.

Finally the talk and eating slowed, grease coagulated on the plates, and the group sank into lethargy. Karen leaned her head on Doug's shoulder, causing Suzanne a pang of jealousy. Myra, astonishingly, fell completely silent; maybe she had nodded off, upright. Suzanne slipped out of her chair and quietly collected dishes. "No, no, just sit," she insisted when Aunt Nelda struggled up. "I could use the exercise." But she let Linda follow her into the kitchen with a stack of plates. They'd talk.

"I'll wash and you dry." Linda rolled up her sleeves and tied one of Suzanne's aprons over her narrow gray skirt.

Suzanne rubbed the dish towel over the pleasantly warm wet plate Linda handed her. "What happened?"

"He decided at the last minute that he didn't want to come. It was too exhausting to meet a bunch of strangers. He'd rather stay home and watch football." She resumed her vigorous scrubbing.

"He's just afraid of commitment," Suzanne said. "Coming to a holiday dinner with you and meeting your friends makes it official."

"Whatever. I've run out of patience. He can never make a plan in advance; he can never decide what he wants to do." Linda put down the bowl she was washing and turned to face Suzanne. "You really think it's fear of commitment?" Suzanne nodded. "God, men are chickenshit, aren't they?"

"They are."

"Good riddance."

"You actually broke up with him? You told him you weren't going to see him again?"

"Uh-huh. You should have seen his face. 'Just because I won't come to one dinner party,' as though we aren't talking about months of this kind of crap. They're such babies. They never expect any consequences from their actions."

"Mark called right at dinner time last Wednesday night and announced he was sleeping at the office. He totally forgot he'd promised to pick up groceries."

"Sounds like he's having an affair to me."

Suzanne straightened. "Of course not. He's had to stay over before. When they have a deadline." Linda wouldn't understand; she'd never been married.

"Whatever. As far as I'm concerned, they're all hopeless."

They worked in silence for a while. "What are you two young ladies up to?" Mark's great aunt had come in behind them and stood leaning on her cane. "Sneaking away to do all the work."

"Aunt Nelda, you go keep Myra company." Suzanne accompanied her back to the dining room. But the party had reawakened.

"Next course." Doug laughed and stretched.

"You didn't wash all the dishes yourself," Maria protested.

"There's plenty for everyone to do," Suzanne answered. "I need help with the coffee and dessert."

As she herded them to their tasks, she saw herself at twelve. That year her grandmother was sick and her mother had stayed at the hospital for hours, leaving Suzanne in charge of Christmas. "Queen Suzanne," Kenny had called her. She remembered the way it stung. An ache had opened in the back of her head and all her fears that Grandma might die poured through it. She'd turned and slapped him in the face, surprising herself because she never fought. That was a mistake; he was stronger and their father wasn't home. He hit her back hard, on the arm, and she'd screamed, outraged at the injustice of it. She did *all* the work and he didn't have to obey her.

"Well, dear, we've all done our duty, except Mark, that is," Myra interrupted her thoughts. "I don't know how you put up with him."

And who waited on him hand and foot when he was growing up? Suzanne thought. "That's all right, Myra; I'll get down the sugar and creamer and we'll be ready for dessert." She found the bowl and pitcher in the back of the cabinet and joined the group at the table. She poured coffee, cut pies, and ate with the others, but remained quiet, half sunk in that cold Christmas when she had felt so frightened and grown up.

After the guests had all gone, carrying the packets of leftovers she'd urged on them, she swept and piled the last of the dishes in the sink. The house was so quiet now. It felt like her birthday when she was a child. The day was enormous, anticipated forever. But then it was over, the cake reduced to a ring of icing on a cardboard square, the presents opened, the wrappings crumpled on the floor, Kenny squabbling with Carol over the favors, and she once again the older sister who had to try to make them stop.

She dumped the pile of bones on the platter into the compost bin. Where was Mark? She wanted his company. She wanted to tell him about Karen and Doug.

She climbed the stairs and there he was, back in front of the tube. "Oh hi," he said, "good dinner." He waved for her to be quiet as he leaned forward to catch the sportscaster's remark.

"Mark, Karen says..."

"Huh? Shush a second."

It was hopeless. He hadn't even turned to look at her. She pressed a hand against the ache in her chest.

Anne

"Round yon virgin, mother and child," the words that went with the tinkling music in the mall came into Anne's head. She thought of her mother's crèche in the corner of the living room. Her father had hated it. But Anne had liked to lie with her head on the cool wood floor and look up past Mary's blue robe and into her face. Mary was pale, dark-haired, and pretty — like her mother but with a secretive smile on her lips.

"God, I hate this Christmas carol Muzak," Mark complained.

"Why?"

"It's schlock. And it made me feel left out when I was a kid. Like the whole world is Christian and we all love to hear this shit blaring out everywhere we go."

"My father said the same thing."

"Smart man."

She sipped her lemonade. Christmas made her feel left out too. She'd never understood it. The fast food section of the mall was so crowded. The air was loud and stuffy with the music, everyone's breathing using it up, and the teenagers calling to each other. Why were all these people and their packages slumped in the white plastic chairs? The dark-haired woman, sitting at the next table in a bright red coat and a red and green scarf, looked drained. Two big shopping bags rested on the seats to either side of her. Her children, Anne thought, imagining the woman leaning to kiss each bag with her berry-red lips.

"Onward?" Mark asked. She nodded. He'd asked her to help him pick a present for his mother.

They strolled through the crowd. Mark took Anne's hand and swung it in his. He stopped in front of a window. "Nice suit. Probably about twelve hundred. If I didn't have a mortgage."

"You'd buy that?" The brown suit looked like any other, boxy and drab.

"Sure, if I could. You gotta treat yourself sometimes."

He moved on. "So what would you want for

Chanukah if you were a sixty-four year old yenta with expensive tastes?"

"My mother likes jewelry." Anne pointed to the window of the next store.

"I bet mine would too. But I wasn't thinking that expensive."

"She likes crystal too."

"Now, that might be more in my price range." Mark squeezed her hand. "But, hey, if I were getting her something here, what do you think would be good?"

Anne studied the display. Her mother always said you should avoid ostentation in jewelry. Antiques were best. But all the pieces here were new. There was a small garnet brooch with tiny pearls on each side of the stone that her mother would approve of. "That one, I think."

"Which, the pin? Yeah, it's pretty. Well, let's find that crystal."

In the shop, light glinted off the faceted surfaces, a shrill clanging. She imagined her mother's perfume bottles flying off the vanity, knocking each other with loud clinks. The amber liquid spilled around her, bright and ringing.

"I have to get out of here."

"Huh? What? You all right?"

"Dizzy."

"Here." He led her to a bench in front of the store. "Put your head between your knees." Darkness slid over her, pulsing. "Better?" he asked in a while.

"Uh–huh."

He held her shoulder and guided her up. "God damned canned air. Just sit for a while; I'll be right back."

She leaned against the wood of the bench. The music crowded the air, circling her head like a halo. Legs bumped past her, beating time. The window of the crystal store winked like an enormous diamond. Too bright, loud. She closed her eyes, sinking into the green needles of a tree. *The shiny ornaments wheeled by her; the lights blinked on and off. But the needles were cool, quiet. She climbed slowly, branch by branch. At the top she stopped, balancing on the prickly stalk, and spread her wings.*

"Hey Annie." She opened her eyes. Mark sat beside her on the bench. "Look. For my Mom. Ta-da!" He pulled a large crystal bowl out of a bag and she recoiled, shielding her eyes, "and for you." He thrust a small box at her. "Come on, open it."

She pulled the lid off slowly, afraid it might explode into a dazzle of light. A square of white cotton inside. Snow. He was giving her snow for Chanukah. She lifted it. Beneath lay the pin from the jewelry store window.

Her first thought was Mommy would be glad. Then she realized it was for her.

"No," she slapped the lid back on the box, "you shouldn't give this to me."

"Don't worry; I put it on plastic."

"It's not for me."

"Why not, because I'm married?" Mark shifted his legs. "Look, I've decided. I'm leaving her."

"No."

"I don't want to go through another holiday like Thanksgiving. I'm getting out of there by Christmas."

"It's not safe."

"To hell with safe, Annie. I'm tired of safe. That's all I ever am with Suzanne." He put a hand on her shoulder. "Look, you don't even have to think about this. It's my business. Come on, let's see how it looks." He pinned the brooch near her throat.

Anne froze. Snow all around her. She had to

escape. "I want to go home."

"Already? Aren't you getting anything for your Mom?"

An idea. She'd send the pin to Mommy. A present from Daddy. She never wanted to divorce him right after he gave her jewelry. "I think I have something."

"O.K., I've had about all I can take of this Christmas music anyway." 'Jingle Bells' followed them out the door.

When they got home, her body wasn't hungry. It stayed but paid no attention when he kissed her. They must not get divorced. They must not get divorced. The words drummed. Mark stopped, held her at arm's length, and peered into her face. "Hey, what's going on? You all right, babe?"

"No."

"What's wrong?...You still dizzy?"

She nodded.

He stroked her cheek. "Poor babe, you might be coming down with something. You should have gotten a flu shot; I get one every year. Go right to bed now, and you might be able to fight it off."

He walked her into the bedroom and pulled

back the covers. "Now you get some rest."

"O.K."

After he left, she sank into bed, falling through the needles of the tree. Voices jangled. They must not get divorced. Holy night. Deck the halls. Lights flashed by. Round yon virgin, mother divorced. No. She pulled herself branch by branch into waking.

You need her. Don't let her.

How? What can I do?

Hold her. Stop her.

Where can I find her?

Fly away home.

Home? Her mother had been at home. Anne remembered a time she'd hurried up the path after the school bus dropped her off. She had something to show her — a picture or a spelling test, something she'd done well on. She'd burst in the door and run to the living room where her mother lay reading on the couch. "That's nice, dear. Put it down there." Mommy's pale hand waving toward the coffee table had flown through the air, an angel so beautiful Anne had wanted to grab and kiss it before it swooped down to land again at her side.

She needed Mommy. They must not get divorced.

Suzanne

Mark thumped down the stairs and Suzanne looked up from her tea to see him holding his briefcase, ready for work. "You're leaving early," she said. "Don't you want any coffee?"

His face stiffened. "No. I want to tell you. I've decided. I want a divorce."

"What?"

"I want a divorce. I don't want to continue this marriage any longer."

"Mark, you're over-reacting to something. What is it?"

"I'm not. I told you; I want a divorce."

She rose, her arm reached out to him, and she drew it back to her side. "Are you crazy? You can't just..."

"I can. I'm going to work now. We'll talk later."

She stood staring at the door he'd left through. He couldn't mean it. She walked slowly to the closet, pulled down her coat, took her purse and book-bag from the hall table where she'd set them the night before, and slowly turned the doorknob. Sun streamed on her garden. The plants in pots on the patio looked so bright: purple lobelia, late snapdragons, gerbera with petals so neat they seemed fake. Her feet took her to her car. He couldn't mean it. He was just being moody. But she felt light-headed, her hands on the steering wheel far away. She braked at a stop sign and didn't go again until someone honked behind her. She turned the corner and drove back slowly, afraid she couldn't navigate the familiar streets. When she stepped out of the car, the sun was so brilliant she stumbled and clutched the door, feeling as though she might faint. But she steadied herself to climb the steep steps past her garden, got the key into the lock on the second try, and called in sick. Her voice echoed oddly in her head.

She had to call him, to talk some sense into him. She could probably reach him at work in fifteen minutes. She started for the table to clear her breakfast things, stopped, stood in the center of the room, turned, walked into the living room, and folded herself onto the couch. The window was full of sky. Below it, houses filled valleys and rose up hills, then the bay, more houses, hills without houses, the peaks of mountains. The scene seemed too bright and substantial to contain any part of her life.

She had to get up. To call him. But, when she did, Adele said he'd be at a meeting all morning, maybe through lunch. She'd have him phone as soon as he got in. Suzanne wondered if it were pity she heard in her voice.

She stood by the phone. Do something. Go to work? But they'd already have called a sub. She closed her eyes and rubbed her temples, trying to push away the confusion. She thought of the vegetable garden she'd wanted to put in the back, in the space she hadn't cleared yet. She'd kept waiting for Mark to help her. She headed out into the glare of the world.

She hacked at the fennel — impossible to pull it out; she'd have to get the roots later. Then started on the Bermuda grass. Each clump had long shallow roots which led to another, so it took her around the plot in a crazy connect-the-dots pattern. On the way she pulled out dandelions though some broke at the base. When the weeds were mostly cleared, she used a small hoe to turn over the soil, working on whatever Bermuda grass was left and slicing the fennel roots — thick, white, and pointed — down as far as she could.

Once in a while she stopped and gazed at the dark inside the door she had left open, thinking it was past lunch time. He should have called by now. Maybe she ought to try him again. But she was tired. It was easier to continue stooping, stretching her arm to weed and hoe, than to straighten, feeling the ache in her back, and walk into the dark.

And what point was there in calling him, talking through wires to a voice in another world? He wasn't himself; she should wait till he calmed down. She'd stay here in the garden, her work in her hands.

Then the phone rang and she rose to her feet to search for it in the grass. She was out of breath when she found it. "Hello." There was no answer. "Hello?"

A woman's voice. "I'm Anne." She stopped. Suzanne heard her breathing on the line. "You don't know me. He told me he wants to divorce you."

"What? Who is this?"

"Please don't divorce him. Please. I don't want him." She hung up.

Suzanne put down the phone. She started toward the stairs to Mark's study, meaning to break something. Instead she swung around, fell onto the couch face first, sobbed once, then lay still.

A memory tugged. She was nine, the winter she had bronchitis. Her illness held her flat in her bed, her limbs too heavy to move. She was in a cave of white: the sheet, the white tufted bedspread, the walls. The snow kept falling outside, the only thing moving. Far away, through a tunnel of fever, her mom clattered in the kitchen. The snow fell from a white sky to a white ground. There was so much of it that she decided it circled in great spirals between heaven and earth. It seemed a momentous discovery. She should tell her mother. She had to get up. She saw herself setting out to call her: the slow steps down the hall, her bare feet on the cold wood, the toppling height at the head of the stairs as though she were in the stars looking down at the lights of the earth. Dark seemed to fall abruptly as she thought this. She was still in her bed; the lamp lit beside her. Her mouth opening, but no sound coming out.

And she didn't have to tell her mother because she knew. This was the secret the grown-ups kept: the endless repeating of the world, nothing wasted, nothing lost, all rocked in the spiral of wind. This was the reason that they didn't cry. They knew everything would return to them.

How important that had seemed to her at nine. She held onto it now in the darkened room as she pulled herself up. She sat for a while, watching the glow of other people's windows. She was comforted. Not the kind of comfort that brings joy or even relief from sorrow, only the willingness to get up, turn on the lamp, do whatever needed to be done.

She walked to the kitchen. When she pushed the switch, the room burst into light. She held her dirty hands under the kitchen tap. The water flowed over them, changing from cold to hot. She felt her skin warm slowly, blood beating in response to the pulsing water. The world circled around the moment and she was present and was calm.

She turned off the water when it got too hot
and walked to the refrigerator, opened it, stood
looking in at the chilly whiteness. Then she focused on an orange, the cheddar cheese. She took
them out, got a knife, sliced cheese onto a napkin, tore into the orange skin with her fingers, releasing the smell of orange peel, a wisp of colored
dust curling toward her nostrils. Smelling it, her
mind was empty of everything else.

So this is my salvation, she thought. This is
the world continuing.

Gray light seeped between the curtains and half
woke Suzanne. Was it morning? She rolled to
look at the clock: 6:49. She'd forgotten to set the
alarm. Mark wasn't there. He hadn't come home
last night. He was with her: the woman on the
phone. How could he?

She held a fist to her chest to push down a sob.
She couldn't let this happen to her. She swung her
legs over the edge of the bed, found her slippers
with her feet, and shuffled to the bathroom. Then
she was slumped on the toilet seat looking at the
toothbrush in her hand. Snap out of it, she told
herself, you're already running late. You can't call

in sick again. She slid to the floor, where she lay curled on the bathroom rug, crying.

She had to leave for work without a shower or breakfast, but when she got there, her mind quieted. She focused on the children. There was a way that, despite all their energy, they were more restful than adults. When Jaime grabbed all of the buttons Joshua was counting for math, she swung into motion, soothed, and restored order in a flurry of quiet words and pats. Then she switched off again, leaned against the wall, and looked out over the classroom.

She felt something soft under her hand. Noni had nestled up to her. Suzanne stroked her sleek head, and the child pressed her companionable warmth against her until Suzanne became a teacher again and asked, "Want to show me your project?"

She could handle this. It was going home she dreaded. And soon she was in her car, turning her wheels into the curb, staring up past her garden at the house with a fear — what if he isn't there? What do I do then?

But of course he wouldn't be there. He always got home later than she did. She drew a long breath and walked up the stairs, then stood on the stoop, reluctant to open the door. The problem was, she realized, that she didn't know if he were coming. I'll call and ask, she thought, and turned the key in the lock.

She hesitated holding the telephone in her hand. What would she say? How should she talk to him now? Just ask him calmly if he were coming home. That was simple enough. She practiced speaking the sentence aloud and dialed.

He wasn't there; Adele didn't know if he'd be back in the office today. He didn't answer his cell when she tried it. She walked to the closet to hang up her jacket and stood staring into it. The coats had no smell. She remembered hiding in the coat closet when she was small and how strong the smell was then — of mothballs, damp wool, winter.

She climbed the stairs to the study. Each step seemed to lift her a little into the air as though she were being pushed. Light glazed the surface of his big desk under the south window. It looked as though she would plunge her hand into water, but the top drawer felt substantial enough. She had to tug to open it. There right in the center, the leather-bound diary she had given him for his birthday. She leafed back a few weeks and found it, written in his cramped handwriting: Anne Bloch, 843-0917, 139 Crossways Avenue, Apt. 6.

If she called that would warn him. She'd have to go there and take him by surprise. 843 was an East Bay exchange; he hadn't written the 510 area code. She found Crossways in Berkeley. She'd better leave before the traffic got bad.

She stood for a while in front of 139 when she arrived. It was a small white apartment building. A box with deco touches around the windows and doorway. More modest than the large single-family houses down the street. She climbed the front steps and found the doorbell for #6 — the last apartment, must be on the top floor — and rang it. The buzzer droned; she pushed the heavy door and started up.

A small woman stood in the doorway of six. She was wearing a gauzy orange blouse, which looked as though it had been expensive but now had an unmended tear at the hem. Her short brown hair curled around her face.

"Who are you?" she asked.

"Suzanne."

The woman grasped the doorjamb as though bracing herself for a blow. "I tried not to."

Then Suzanne realized how foolish she had been. Mark wasn't here. "Oh, forget it," she said. "I didn't come here for you. I was just looking for my stupid husband but apparently he's not here." She waved her arm at the empty apartment.

Anne backed away. "Don't touch it." She stood silently a moment, then spoke, "I'm having trouble with my body." She leaned against the door, half closing it.

"I'm going," Suzanne told her. What was wrong with the woman? How could Mark pick someone like that? She strode to the stairs, hearing the door close behind her.

Anne

Someone was ringing the bell. Mark hadn't
called. Maybe a deliveryman with a present from
her mother. Or it could be Suzanne. She had come
once but hadn't stayed. She was so pretty. Anne
pressed the buzzer to unlock the door. It would be
good to see her again.

"Ho, ho, ho," Mark bounded up the stairs,
"Merry Christmas and all that crap."

Anne felt disappointed. "I didn't know you
were coming."

"A spur of the moment decision. I thought you
might be lonely."

"Why?"

"Well, Christmas and all."

It was Christmas already? She'd forgotten to
send her mother the brooch.

He put a small suitcase down on the couch
and kissed her.

"Glad to see me?'

She studied his bag suspiciously, afraid of another gift. "What's that?"

"Just a few things I thought I'd leave here so I'd have them when I need them."

"Your things?"

"Yeah, like a toothbrush and a change of clothes."

Good, they weren't for her. Mark pulled her down onto the couch. "So how are we going to celebrate this goyish holiday?" he asked. "You hungry? Think any restaurants are open?"

"I don't know."

"Hand me my phone, I'll try."

He made a few calls, muttering,"Damn," in between. "No luck. Got anything in the fridge?"

"No."

"Come on, Annie, I know you eat. Let's see what you've got."

She didn't like him looking at her food and followed him into the kitchen. He crouched in front of the refrigerator. "You eat this shit?" He held out a package of sliced American cheese. He pulled open the vegetable drawer, then closed it quickly. "Oh, a science experiment." He rose and opened the freezer compartment. "Ah ha, Annie, I've discovered your secret: T.V. dinners." She imagined closing the door on him. Would he crack into shards in the cold? But he shut it and turned toward her. "Is your grocery store open? Probably not, right? Should we just take a walk and see what we can find?"

That would get him out of the house. "Yes."

It was cold outside. The world empty, gray. "Why's it so quiet?" she asked him.

"Christmas," he answered. "They're all happy Christians celebrating by unwrapping presents and stuffing themselves. Damn, I hope we can find something open. You know a deli? Maybe a Chinese place?"

"I think the people in the corner store are Korean."

"So we can buy more T.V. dinners while everyone else is eating turkey? Come on, Annie, I want a meal." He strode ahead of her, his hands jammed into his pockets.

At Broadway he stopped and peered down the street. "Hey, Annie, I think we're in luck. Isn't that Thai place open?" He took her hand and shoved it with his into his pocket. "Well babe, food at last."

Why was food so important to him, she wondered as he solemnly studied the menu. They were the only diners in the restaurant, but it was crowded with colors. As she ate, she felt presences pulsing along the edges between red and green, gold and blue. They wanted to talk to her; sit beside her at the table; share her festive, surprising food full of shifts in taste and texture.

Mark talked on about work, plans, places to live. She couldn't hear him very well with all the noise the colors made, but she nodded, said "yes" or "oh" occasionally to keep him from interrupting her as she listened to their humming. "Well, that hit the spot," he said at the end of the meal as he tilted back in his chair. "I feel much better now. Hey Annie," he scrutinized her, "you're not wearing the pin I gave you. No point in having nice stuff if you don't use it."

His face bobbed above the table like a balloon. If she had the pin, she could have pricked him and watched him pop into shreds.

"How can someone who eats so many TV dinners live without a TV?" he said when they returned to her apartment. "You should get one,

Annie."

No. She wouldn't allow a noisy box in her place. Her body bumped him. He was taking up too much space.

He turned and pulled her to him. "All right, babe, that's even better."

She rubbed against him. Maybe her body could eat him, at least take a few bites to make him smaller.

But afterwards, she still felt hungry, restless. She got up and stretched her arms toward the ceiling. "Hey babe," Mark called languidly from the bed, "can you bring me my bathrobe from the suitcase?"

She found it on the sofa. Inside were jeans, some white shirts, men's underwear, a bathroom kit, and the wine-colored robe. Was he going on a trip? No, he said he was leaving these here.

She handed him the bathrobe. "That's too much stuff. You better take some of it home."

"Annie, I don't have a home. I'm staying in a hotel." He folded the robe on the chair by the bed.

"But what about the house with the garden?"

He turned toward her. "I can't just throw her out."

She felt scared. "That's your house. It isn't right."

"Shush, Annie, I'm sleepy." He flopped onto his back. "We can talk about it tomorrow. Come to bed, would you, babe?"

He had to go back to his house. She should have known the suitcase was dangerous. Every time her father went on a trip, her mother said maybe she wouldn't let him come back. He could just go live with "Her." What if Daddy left with a suitcase and never came back? Would Mommy leave too? Would she be all alone?

Suzanne

"You should have told me." Karen sounded hurt.

Suzanne studied her friend across the table. The pregnancy didn't show yet, but she looked softer, rounder. In contrast Suzanne felt like a paper cut-out: angular and flat.

"I'm sorry, Karen," she answered. "I couldn't bring myself to call anyone."

"I know. And I've been so exhausted I haven't called you in ages. But I just don't understand it. It's so sudden. He didn't give you any reason at all?"

Karen looked so distressed that Suzanne had a disloyal thought: she's afraid it could happen to her. "No, he's hardly spoken to me," she answered. She couldn't tell her about Anne. It made such an odd picture of herself — the spurned, jealous wife.

"Oh Suzanne, I'm sorry, I shouldn't make you

talk about it. I just can't believe he'd do that." She reached across the table and took Suzanne's hand. "Come to dinner tomorrow? If I'm tired, I can sleep in Saturday."

"All right. Thank you. But let me pay for this."

Her legs felt heavy as she headed up the hill toward home. Maybe she had avoided Karen because it seemed so strange to be meeting her for lunch as though everything were the same. And nothing was. Even from the sidewalk, looking up at her house, she could feel its emptiness. She trudged up the steps with the sound of her grandmother singing 'Put on a happy face' rattling in her head. Then 'Hail, hail, the gang's all here.' They had sung that when they visited, and Suzanne remembered how angry she'd been when Kenny changed 'What the heck do we care' to 'What the fuck do we care.' She'd shushed him furiously, hoping that Grandma hadn't heard and been hurt.

The house was so quiet. Would there ever be anyone to keep her company again? She went to wash her hands in the kitchen sink, hoping for the comfort the warm water had brought her that first night without Mark. But it was just water and her hands felt numb. She opened the refrigerator door. Nothing to snack on. It seemed too much of an effort to cook a whole meal; she wasn't really hungry. She had a few lesson plans to prepare and might as well get started. But on the way she drifted into the living room and stood in the dark, looking out at the view. The hills were specked with lights: large ones near her and smaller ones, more beautiful in their delicacy, farther away. Like Christmas all year round, her father had said when her parents visited, the year before he died. And now she'd spent Christmas alone in the house. She'd been so happy when they'd bought it. She'd slept on the couch the first night so she could see the view whenever she opened her eyes. Mark had teased her about buying a house and losing a wife. The bastard. She slid to her knees in front of the couch, pounding it with her fists.

She wondered if the neighbors could hear and quieted, laying her cheek against the brocade. How could he? Pull yourself together. She raised her head from the damp cloth and wiped her eyes, then walked up the stairs slowly, and spread out her papers on her desk.

Later the phone rang. "It's Linda. Just saying hi. How are you doing?"

"All right."

"Come on, Suzanne, stop trying to be the woman of steel. You're not all right, no one would be all right with what that crazy bastard did."

"You told Karen."

"Yeah, I figured she should know. You need all the support you can get. You're not mad, are you? She *is* an old friend."

"No. I was just surprised. You hardly know her."

"I checked information, sweetheart, anything for you. So how are you doing for the weekend? Any plans?"

"I'm going to Karen and Doug's for dinner to-morrow."

"Good. So would you come shopping with me Saturday? Downtown? We can splurge on the good stuff."

"I'll watch you splurge. Why get dressed up for five-year-olds? They just barf or spill paint all over you."

"But what if you have a hot date?"

"Linda, why would I have a date?"

"Girl, why wouldn't you have a date? There's plenty of men out there with their tongues hanging out for you. What was that one at work you told me about — Michael? It sounds like he'll be knocking on your door as soon as he finds out you're available."

"He's ten years younger than me. And besides, I'm still married."

"So's Mark. You don't owe him anything, girl."

Suzanne felt an urge to defend Mark out of old loyalty but couldn't think of anything to say. "I guess so," she replied.

"You know, there are some single guys I work with. I could introduce you. Just to get you out of the house. You don't have to take them seriously."

"Linda, thanks. But I can't even think about that now."

"Well anytime you're ready. And call anytime, too. Don't be so damn stoic. See you Saturday then. Should I come by about eleven?"

"All right. See you then."

"See you."

Talking to Linda was no better than to Karen, Suzanne thought and then felt guilty. But they didn't understand. As though I'd want to go out with some stranger. Her chest tightened. Would she really have to go on dates, look for another man? Michael? She shook her head. Ridiculous. She supposed he did flirt with her, and he was overly affectionate, putting an arm around her shoulder when they passed each other in the hall. But she had dismissed it as a crush. He was too young to know what he wanted, just out of school.

That's older than Mark and I were when we met, she realized. But that was different. Why? Maybe the time that had passed since then made it different, all the years she and Mark had spent growing used to each other.

A shocking loneliness washed over her. For a moment she thought of calling Linda back. But no, Linda had to work early tomorrow, and what was there to say? She rose slowly, her back and legs stiff.

The next day was gray, cold, and felt like winter. At five it was dark already and Suzanne had hardly started shearing the rockroses. She stood, pressing her hands into the small of her back. Christmas vacation would be over soon. There was so much left to do and now she had no more light.

She shook her head, annoyed that she was about to cry. She had to get ready for dinner at Karen and Doug's anyway. She didn't really want to go, but maybe it was good to have something to do. She stooped to gather her tools, feeling dizzy as she rose, and headed in.

She lay in the tub, looking down at her body, flushed from the hot water. Could it really be over? What if she were alone for the rest of her life? She put her head on her knees, feeling sweat from the steam trickle down the back of her neck. It couldn't last with Anne. Did she want him back? Would he want her? What questions. She had never imagined she'd be asking these questions.

The phone rang. She wrapped a towel around herself and went to answer it.

"Suzanne?" A woman's voice.

"Yes?"

"You've got to stop him; he wants to stay here."

What? "Is this Anne?"

"Yes."

This is sick, she thought. Now I'm involved with my husband's girlfriend. "Look, why are you calling me?"

"I don't want him here. I don't want him staying overnight."

"That's your problem." He wasn't staying there?

"He should be with you."

The sorrow she felt at that made her angry. "What if I don't want him?"

"Don't say that. I want you to be together."

"And I assume you've told him about this desire of yours?"

"He never listens."

"I guess you need to be a little more emphatic."

"He left some clothes and stuff here. I don't want them. Can you take them home?"

Was she asking her to go there? Why? "What good would that do?"

"They shouldn't be here. They scare me."

"So give them back to him if you don't want them. Why are you involving me?"

"I can't stand it any longer. It's too crowded. If you don't come I'll have to throw them out. They might be important."

"That doesn't concern me in the slightest."

"Come tonight. You came here before."

And that was obviously a mistake. But it was on the way to Karen's. And it was better than having Anne show up on her doorstep with the stuff, if Mark had been stupid enough to give her the address. "Oh all right. Have it ready."

"I will." Anne hung up without saying goodbye.

Damn Mark for getting her into this, Suzanne thought as she put down the phone. But he wasn't there on a Friday night. She'd known it wouldn't last. He couldn't even handle his mistress without her help.

Now she'd have to rush. She dried off quickly and combed her hair. Her face in the mirror looked calm, her eyes their usual gray-blue, unmarked by the tears. In the bedroom she pulled on her jeans, then took them off and searched in the closet for the wool dress that matched her eyes. In the back, a little wrinkled, but it would be fine once she got it out of the closet and wore it a while. She found tights and tugged on her boots. Dresses were such a bother.

She started downstairs, then turned back, rummaged in her top drawer for her grandmother's sapphire necklace and attached the clasp at the back of her neck.

Better get going, she told herself. Downstairs, she reached for the closest coat in the closet. She locked up and started the car, trying not to think about how foolish she'd been to get dressed up for Anne.

Traffic wasn't too bad. There was one stall on the bridge, and she put on lipstick in the mirror waiting for the cars to start moving again. "You're losing it, Suzanne," she said out loud and then felt even crazier for talking to herself.

She recognized the apartment building and parked, amazed at herself for coming here. The first time especially. That's what had given Anne the idea. What had she been thinking of? She hadn't been thinking at all, she realized; she'd been in shock. Well this is the last time, she promised, to give herself the momentum to step out of the car. If Anne found any more of Mark's belongings around the place, she'd have to come to the city and meet her at a restaurant.

Anne's door was open when Suzanne reached the third floor. She knocked on the frame and waited while Anne walked slowly in from the back, wearing the same ripped orange blouse.

"Where's the stuff?" Suzanne asked.

"I'm sorry I made you come all this way, but Mark can't help me."

"Help you what?"

"I don't like divorce."

"You might have thought of that earlier."

"Don't divorce him."

"It's his choice."

"Don't."

"Look, if you don't want him, why don't you just break up with him?"

"My body won't let me."

Suzanne stiffened. "Well, I guess you'll just have to make up your mind," she said coldly.

"No, it's not me," Anne's voice was panicked. "It's you and him."

"Look, you're going to have to talk to him yourself; I can't do it for you. I just came here to get those things and go."

"Don't say it's me. I didn't tell him to get divorced. I told him not to." Anne picked up a suitcase and thrust it toward her. "Here. I didn't ask for them. You can't say it's me. You can't divorce him because of me."

"I don't see what you want me to do."

"Promise you won't divorce him."

"I can't promise you anything. Goodbye."

The suitcase tugged at her hand on the way back to the car. She wanted to look inside it, imagining that she'd learn some secret about Mark. Find out how he'd managed to hide from her so well the fact that he could live without her. But Anne might be watching from her window. She loaded the bag onto the passenger's seat, started the car, drove two blocks, and pulled to the curb.

She unlatched the clasp and gazed into the jumble of jeans and underwear. It could have been any man's clothes. She reached in, searching for something familiar, and pulled out his maroon velour bathrobe. He'd had it for years. She held it up to her face. But it didn't smell like him; it didn't smell like anyone at all.

She had to stop crying. She had to be at Karen's and Doug's soon. She didn't want to go with red eyes.

Anne

It hadn't worked, Anne thought sadly. Suzanne had left before Mark arrived. She curled on the sofa, pulling her knees to her chest. She remembered her mother lying on her satin couch complaining about her father. She had been beautiful like Suzanne but with dark hair instead of light. When she'd raised her arm over her eyes, her bracelets had clicked and her perfume had stirred, heavy and strange, like the orchid in the corner when it bloomed once a year. That had made her mother happy. "Come see, it's blooming," she would call to Anne, who always went to admire it because her father didn't. "He ignores me," her mother had fretted in her soft voice. "I really should divorce him. Violet says she saw him with 'Her' at La Maison Thursday. He doesn't even have the dignity to hide it." She'd stretched both arms above her head; the bracelets had jangled, "but then how would I have the money to take care of you?"

Anne had wanted to put her hands over her mother's mouth when she heard that, but Mommy didn't like her to muss her make-up. So she'd held her fingers in her ears, but soon she was tempted and took them out. Her mother's voice enthralled her. "Darling, it's impossible to be a woman," she had said. "We're always at their mercy. They can't stand it when we get old, even though they are too." She fussed all the time about being old; she thought that was why Daddy saw "Her." But Anne had met her, and she wasn't pretty like Mommy. Once when Anne and Daddy went to the zoo, she was there waiting on a bench and came up. Daddy put one arm around her and one around Anne and introduced her. Her name was Millie. She had a square face, short hair, and flat shoes. She swung her arms when she walked and laughed loudly. She gave Anne some sourballs and a coloring book, and Anne remembered to say thank you even though she was too old for coloring and didn't like the candy.

Anne hadn't known how to tell her mother that she didn't need to worry about Millie when

she was so much more beautiful. She'd suspect-
ed Mommy would be angry that Anne had seen
her and she hadn't. Suzanne was pretty too. Why
couldn't they all be together — Mark, Suzanne,
and Anne, like Daddy, Mommy, and Anne?

The doorbell. Heavy steps on the stairs. Mark
burst in. "Whew, what a day." He leaned down to
kiss her. "Let me change, and then do you want to
go out for dinner or just get take-out?"

She heard him rummaging in her closet. "Hey
Annie, where'd you put my jeans?"

"Suzanne took them."

"What?" He rushed back into the living room.
"Did you say Suzanne?"

"Yes."

He took two steps toward her and stood in the
center of the room. "Annie, what the hell is going
on?" Then his voice calmed and he slumped into
the chair in the corner. "Tell me exactly what happened. Did she come here? How did she get the
address?"

"I called her."

"What?"

"I don't want you to get a divorce. Suzanne

says maybe you won't."

"What the fuck does she have to say about it?" He walked to the window, stared out, then turned and glared at her. "Or you too, for that matter."

Anne imagined his angry face bobbing like a balloon on his neck. She didn't like him shouting in her living room. Then he unclenched his fists and lowered his voice. "I'm sorry I yelled at you, Annie. I know Suzanne can be really pushy, but I just want to know why she came here."

"So you could talk to her."

"Well I don't want to. And don't let her come again, no matter what she says." He looked at her sternly. "From now on stay away from her. If she calls, let me handle it."

"Why do you *have* to get divorced?"

He leaned against the wall, gazed out the window again, then turned back. "Let's drop it, O.K.? I'm tired; I had a hard day. I don't want to think about Suzanne." He was silent for a moment, then walked over to her and pulled her up from the couch into a hug. He leaned his chin on the top of her head. "Come on, Annie, you're the one I want to think about now."

Her body reached her arms around his back.

He leaned down to kiss her forehead, then her mouth.

In the bed, he undressed her slowly, stopping to kiss her skin as the clothes came off. She waited for her body to clench as he moved inside it, but nothing happened. She was tired, impatient for it to be over.

Daddy can't help you. Her body talking. *I told you, forget about him. He always ignores us. That's what Mommy said.*

She wanted Mommy. She'd looked so soft and smooth that Anne had found it hard to remember not to touch her. Once she'd poked her finger up into the top of a pleat on her skirt, and her mother had pushed her hand away with a sharp gesture. Her clothes were soft and her pale skin underneath looked even softer. Anne stroked Mark's back, imagining he was her mother. If Mommy would just let her hug her, wrap her arms around her legs and nestle her face in her skirt, which smelled like baby powder. Touch her face, trace the dark eyebrows with her fingertips, pat the pink, shiny lips. Sometimes wisps of her hair were curled damply against her long neck, and Anne wanted to wrap them around her finger. Her finger in Mark's hair. Her body grabbed, floated. She fell asleep imagining that Mommy held her, kissed her cheeks and eyelids.

Suzanne

Suzanne had the day off. She stretched her legs, feeling the familiar pang at the emptiness on the other side of the bed. But at least it wasn't a weekend when she woke up missing Mark. If Karen or Linda hadn't invited her somewhere, she'd have preferred to stay home rather than see all the couples wandering hand in hand around the city. A day off when Mark was at the office had always been a chance for her to work on her own projects. She hurried through breakfast, thinking of what she might do. She wanted to go out. The park? She'd see what was blooming in the arboretum; she needed ideas for flowering perennials to plant in the back among the vegetables.

She sat on the edge of the stone circle just inside the arboretum entrance and ran her hand over the thyme, then held her fingers to her nose. There was no smell. It disappointed her. Don't be silly, she told herself. To her right, magnolias bloomed — huge white cups against bare branches — and she walked toward them. She found herself reading the plaques: Magnolia 'Grace McDade,' Magnolia 'Ann,' with purple buds; then further on Magnolia salicifolia 'Wada's Memory' with long white petals drooping from the tips of its branches. Who were these women the trees were named for? Wives? Lovers? Perhaps the horticulturist herself. That thought cheered her. She imagined leaning over a flower, carefully brushing the pistil with pollen from a basting tube. Was that how it was done? She had no idea.

She passed the rough stone monument commemorating the visit of the Emperor and Empress of Japan. She bent to touch the dainty leaves of the Artemis frigida from Siberia, wondering if it grew in the snow. She sniffed her fingers for the wormwood smell but it was muted: faint, like the day, like her calm melancholy. She stopped at a bench, then read its plaque: "Martha Trammell/ Love is Eternal." She didn't want to cry, so stood again, walked past a pond green with algae, dark wintry rocks standing in the water, like indecipherable emotions. In the cloud forest there were tall trees, a sense of height, mountains, but it was too shady. She needed light.

In the Cape Province section, she saw that the Anisodontea was in bloom. It reminded her of her purpose here, and she thought it would fit well in a sunny corner of her vegetable garden. She rubbed a leaf of Pelargonium crispum and savored the strong lemon scent. It made her think of the orange peel that had brought her comfort. That's what she wanted — smells. She would go to the Fragrance Garden.

She found it around a curve in the path. First the sages. Their variety pleased her: Salvia spathacea, pitcher sage, with its huge leaves; Salvia clevelandii, narrow leaves and a pungent citrusy smell; Salvia sonomensis 'Dara's Choice,' humble, low to the ground, but someone had valued it enough to choose it from the wild and bring it into cultivation.

She rubbed the leaves of the mints, the chamomile, the thymes. Familiar smells, strong and invigorating. The European wormwood, Artemis absinthum, was delicious, and smelled like food. Then the Culinary Herb section: rosemary, fennel, garlic chives, lovely oregano, and two kinds of parsley — curly leaf and Italian. She smiled, happy with an idea: she'd cook an elaborate dinner for Linda and Karen. Should she invite Doug too? She probably ought to, a thank you for their support. Something festive and difficult. Julia Child's leg of lamb with a head of garlic plunged into boiling water over and over? Or goose, she'd always wanted to try that. She strode out of the arboretum feeling purposeful.

On the way home, she stopped at the grocery store to check about ordering goose and pick up a few things. She struggled up the steps with her bags; she'd have to remember to do it in two trips next time. This was too much for one person to carry. She paused, set them down, and put her key in the lock. The door had already been opened. Her breath caught. She leaned in slowly and listened.

"Suzanne?"

Oh my God. It was Mark.

He clattered down the stairs. She hadn't seen him since the morning he'd said he wanted a divorce. Was he back? Had he broken up with Anne? He looked so familiar it was hard to believe he'd been gone.

They both spoke at once: "What...?" / "I thought..."

"Go ahead," she said.

"I thought you were at work."

"School's closed today. It's Martin Luther King's Birthday." He wasn't here to see her.

"Oh." He paused. "I'm just finishing up. I'll be out of your way in a sec." He started back upstairs.

"Wait." The tears she felt angered her. "Why are you here?"

"It doesn't matter."

"You scared me." She held her hand to her chest. "You can't come barging in like this."

"Why not? You do."

"What?"

"I still own this house, you know."

"So? What does that mean?"

"So I can come here if I want."

"Well, you might give me some warning, or I'll have to change the locks."

Mark waved his hand as though batting her words away. "I didn't come here to fight, Suzanne."

"Why did you come then?"

"I'm just picking up some stuff. Let me get it

and I'll be out of here." He strode upstairs.

She stood a minute, then gathered up her groceries. She wouldn't let him ruin her mood when she was finally feeling a little better. A thought ran through her mind: but he looks the same. She put the bags down on the kitchen table, unloaded the perishables. She reached in for a carton of milk, carried it to the refrigerator, opened the door, realized there was another carton, and went back for it still holding the first. He was up there. She put the milk away, closed the refrigerator door, then remembered the cheese. Should she freeze the fish? It was so much better fresh. Cook it tonight? His footsteps above her. Bread into the bread bin, onions into the hanging basket. Leeks? Upstairs Mark began to whistle. She slammed the leeks into the vegetable drawer. She couldn't stay in here any longer. She took her clippers and trowel from the closet and headed into the garden.

She found a dandelion among the lobelia and yanked it out. A snail. She crushed it on the patio. What was taking him so long? Her finger hooked on a thorn in a rose bush, and she sucked away the spot of blood. She really should move some of these lobelia; they were crowding the roses. A plant came out without its roots. She tossed it in the weed bucket and reached for her trowel, stabbing it into the earth beside the next clump of flowers. She didn't like him sneaking around up there. She'd left the letter she was working on to Carol on the desk. She'd been trying to write to her family about the separation. It seemed easier than phoning and having to deal with their response right away. With the trowel she lifted the plant and a ball of dirt. Where should she put it? In the big pot on the patio with the strawberries? She jabbed a hole into the dirt and placed the plant in it. Mark thumped down the front steps, holding the suitcase from Anne's apartment.

"Well bye." He half raised his arm.

She shoved her trowel into the soil. It hit the edge of the pot, jarring her hand.

The suitcase swung as Mark continued down the steps.

He was different. He wasn't her husband: someone known, irritating sometimes with all his familiar faults, but part of her. She had the sensation of splitting in two: the old Suzanne holding out her hand to Mark while the new Suzanne stood aside, watching this tall man who had once been her husband cheerfully trotting down the steps away from their house. She felt something. Not just sorrow for what he used to be. Something else. An old feeling, one that had to do with her brother Kenny. It ticked in the bottom of her feet, rising up her legs. It clenched her hands, tightened her jaw. She was angry. Very angry.

He opened the door of his red BMW. She'd helped him buy that car. Her arm pulled back, then up in an arc, and the trowel sailed out of her hand hitting his tail light with a satisfying crunch.

Mark slowed to a stop, opened the car door, walked to the back, and bent to examine his lights. He stood and shouted something at her. Then he got back in the car and sped around the corner.

Hold your horses, her grandmother's phrase, echoed in her head as she watched him. I didn't hold my horses. She imagined an illustration in a children's book — Arabian stallions, their manes tossing, dashing off in all directions. She pushed a strand of hair behind her ear, walked to the street, and picked up the trowel. She saw a piece of yellow plastic on the asphalt and found herself smiling. I'm acting awfully childish, she thought. She hoped no one had seen her.

Back at her garden she surveyed the rosebushes. Petals had fallen, littering the lobelia. She laid down her trowel, fetched her clippers, and started snipping off the dead flower heads.

Anne

Anne watched Suzanne lift a forkful of salad to her mouth. None spilled. She was so poised. Anne had already dropped two lumps of greasy pasta on her lap. "What grade do you teach?" she asked.

"Grade?" Suzanne looked startled. "Oh, I teach kindergarten."

That seemed right to Anne. She could see her holding hands with a little girl, swinging their arms together as she led her down the sidewalk in front of a procession of children. She must be a good teacher. She imagined the child tugging at her hand, asking to be carried. Suzanne swooped her up. "Do you hug the kids a lot?"

"Sometimes. Look, I thought you had to talk to me about Mark. I only came because you said you had his keys. Where are they?"

"I forgot to bring them. He doesn't matter."

"Then why did you insist we get together? Why are you wasting my time?"

Was she angry? Did she want to talk about Mark? "Why don't you and Mark have kids?"

"For God's sakes, Anne, what's going on here? Mark and I are separated. He had an affair with you."

"Do you want me to stop seeing him?"

Suzanne pushed her hair away from her temples with both hands. "I'm not going to tell you what to do. You're going to have to make up your own mind. And there's no reason to assume we'll get back together if you do stop seeing him. Did it ever occur to you that you may have done too much damage already?"

She was angry. Anne had said the wrong thing. If only her body hadn't made her sleep with Mark, then Suzanne would be her friend. "I don't think he really wants to divorce you," she tried.

"And what gives you that impression?"

"He still loves you."

"He said that to you?"

Suzanne's eyes weren't really blue; they were more a light grey. Her eyebrows were darker than her hair. Mark had said she had wrinkles, but Anne didn't see any. Maybe a few, right in the edges of her eyes and mouth. She leaned closer, and Suzanne turned away. What did she want her to answer? She decided she should say "Yes."

Suzanne pushed her chair back from the table. "Why are you telling me this?"

Her voice sounded so harsh that Anne started. She thought yes had been the right answer. She felt scared.

"Well, why?" Suzanne repeated.

"I was trying to be friends."

"That scarcely seems possible, does it? Considering the circumstances."

"I made a mistake. I'm sorry. I'm telling you I'm sorry."

"That's very generous of you. But it's a little late."

"Can't I do something to make it up?"

"I doubt it."

"I promise never to see him again."

"Suit yourself." Suzanne stood. "I'll get the bill."

Her steps were short and fast; her blond hair swung across her back as she walked. Going away.

Now Anne was alone in a strange restaurant.

Half of Suzanne's salad still sat on her plate. Would she come back to finish it? Should Anne? Some pasta was left too. Eat both? She reached for her fork, but the motion made her dizzy. Pink walls circled around her. She focused on a picture in a gold frame: green and brown hills looming over little people. They pitched on the walls, then steadied. They were safe now, a family alone in the enormous world. If Suzanne would come back, Anne might be safe.

"Should I clear this?"

A waitress stood over her shoulder. Clear what? The dishes. She wasn't going to yell at Anne for not finishing the food. "We're done," she answered.

Soon she was settled in the BART train gazing at her reflection in the window. No one had sat next to her. Still she didn't like taking the train alone. Her mother had tried to make her ride to the city for music lessons. She wouldn't. Suzanne would never do that to her daughter. She'd be a good mother. Would her child have blond hair like hers or dark curly hair like Mark's? Maybe in between, brown curly hair like Anne's. She'd be such a happy little girl. She'd roll in the dirt of the garden, and Suzanne wouldn't care that her clothes got dirty. She could yell in the house and bump on her bottom down the stairs. She wouldn't have to show her daddy her paintings. Mommy would save them in a secret place. If only she could be friends with Suzanne. If Mark hadn't spoiled everything. She was shut out. She always had been scared of the train doors closing in her face, of being left on the platform after dark. Her face in the window floated on the dark of the tunnel, alone.

Suzanne

I must be out of my head, Suzanne thought, driving home. I'm as crazy as she is. Or maybe she wasn't so crazy, saying she had Mark's keys to give her, making it sound as though they'd broken up. They clearly hadn't. But what was the point?

Who cared? What she should be asking was why she allowed it and how had she gotten sucked into this craziness? It must have been morbid curiosity. Her windows were fogging. She rolled the driver's side down, and a raindrop splashed onto her cheek. Damn, she inched the window back up so there was just a crack, then had to brake sharply at the corner. Great, run a stop sign. Get yourself killed.

She drove the rest of the way slowly. Walked slowly up her front steps, stopping, despite the drizzle, to break off the dead flower spikes of the Mexican sage, the leaves releasing a shower of drops onto her hand. In the kitchen she sat at the table in her raincoat, listlessly thinking of making a cup of herbal tea. She didn't feel sad or even angry, only quiet and bemused. Why? Why had she gone to meet Anne? Why had Anne asked her? Why had Mark liked crazy Anne more than her?

She stretched her hands in front of her, rubbed the thin gold wedding band that was not a talisman against disaster. Maybe the answers didn't matter. She remembered that talk with her grandmother when she had complained about some outrage that Kenny had gotten away with because her mother was too tired to deal with it. Grandma had hugged her, then told her firmly, "There's no point in dwelling on it, dearie. Things aren't always fair. Do your best, forget the rest." Pleased with the rhyme, Suzanne had made a song from her grandmother's saying and gone around humming it for days. The tune came back to her now. Things happen, she told herself. There are reasons. But it isn't worth puzzling them all out. One goes on. One does one's best.

Anne

Why was he in her bed, taking up space, snoring? He'd thrown his heavy arm over hers. The rough hairs irritated her skin. Her body was so dumb. It had picked the wrong person. She shoved his arm off and rolled to the edge of the mattress. He grunted, shifted onto his back, but didn't wake up. She turned on the lamp. Still sleeping. He was too big. His feet made a bump at the bottom of the bed. He hogged the center. She swung out of bed and left the room.

Some light in the living room. The trapped tree poked a branch at the side window. The world milky, thick. As though while she slept it had vanished and she floated in this soup. She stared at the east.

A speck appeared. It sailed toward her. She saw colors in it now: red, yellow, blue. People standing in a balloon. It was almost to the window, and she recognized her mother's crèche. Joseph with his red robe; Mary looking sad and beautiful like her mother; and in the manger with its yellow straw, she strained to see as it bumped against the window, the baby. But it wasn't Jesus. It was a girl. The sphere slid through the window; she jumped back, but the pane didn't break. A girl, brown curly hair topped by the gold foil halo. She held her arms out. Suzanne's daughter. Anne reached for her and the balloon broke, colors glinting off the corners of the room.

She ran to the phone and dialed squinting in the half-light. Two rings. "Who is it?"

"It's Anne."

"What's the matter? Is Mark all right?"

"I don't care about him. You're more important."

"Wait a minute. Is everything all right there? No one's hurt?"

"No."

"You just called to talk?"

"Yes."

"Do you know what time it is?"

"No."

"Don't you ever, ever call me at this hour again. Don't you ever call me again at all."

"Suzanne." The dial tone shrilled in her ear. She dropped the phone and slid to the floor. She grasped her knees and rocked. The Jesus girl wrapped in her blanket, gold halo on her curly brown hair. The color sucked out. The world gray. She rocked smaller and smaller until there was nothing.

For a while the world had been shaking. Noises. "N...E, N...E." No, "Annie, Annie." That meant something. Someone's name. She was a person with that name. Someone wanted to talk to her. But it was dark. Open her eyes. A face leaned over her; a hand held her shoulder.

"Annie, are you O.K.?"

Mark.

"Annie, come on. Talk to me."

Talk. She opened her mouth. Where were the words? "Why?"

"What? Annie, what happened? Were you sleepwalking?"

"Why talk to you?"

"Come on, Annie, get back to bed." He pulled

at her, trying to nudge her up.

She sank toward the floor. "I don't want you. I want Suzanne."

Something happened to his face. It shifted, then pulled away. She felt better when it wasn't there, more space. "What the hell are you talking about? What do you mean, you want Suzanne?" The voice came from above her head. She looked up. He stood over her. He seemed unsteady; she wondered if his parts might shift again and fall, the large head tumbling down. She slid out of range.

"I can't be friends with both of you," she said.

"Did Suzanne talk you into this?"

"Suzanne is better for me."

He stared at her. "Jesus Christ. I've had enough."

He moved but his head stayed on. Then he was gone. Safer now. More space. She stretched out on the floor, closing her eyes.

A lion nudged her face, trying to wake her. Hot breath on her cheek. She opened her eyes, sunlight, though she felt the lion leaving, saw out of the corner of her eye the flip of his tail. Everything was crisp and distinct; a blue line ran along the edge of her wrist, which lay on the floor near her head. She lifted her arm and brought it into shadow. That movement started a momentum which carried her to her feet. She felt light and empty. She walked to the kitchen counter, touched its ugly freckles. Mark was gone. Good. But there was something she needed. She opened a cabinet and looked in. A bag of candy fell out. She jumped back as it hit the counter. It didn't appeal to her now. Something light, sandy like the lion. Suzanne. Now that Mark was out of the way, she had to find Suzanne.

She stood, brought her hand to her mouth and bit her thumb. She had to be careful. She'd said the wrong things the last times. She couldn't do that again. She stretched her arms above her head to clear it. She'd go to her tree and swing; that would help her think.

Its leaves had all fallen. It was brave, standing there with its skeleton exposed.

She reached out her hand. The bark felt rough, cool. She grabbed the branch, hung, swaying. Nothing happened; she didn't feel any different except that her arms were tired. Gravity tugged at her weight; her arms strained; the bark dug into her skin. She dropped to the ground. She was in her body. She realized she was always in her body now.

She wasn't sure if this were good or bad. Look at all the mistakes it had made with Mark and Suzanne. Ask the tree? It knew her body better than anyone, except maybe Mark, and she didn't want to talk to him.

She leaned against it, rubbed its bark with her cheek, ran her hands up and down its trunk. Mark had wanted her to do that. "Should I stay in my body?" she asked.

"You don't have any choice."

"Is it dangerous?"

"It doesn't matter."

"What do I do now?"

"Whatever you want."

"Whatever I want? Anything at all?"

"Yes."

She walked away through the fallen leaves. How would she know what she wanted to do? Her body would tell her.

Inside she took off all her clothes and sat on the couch. She watched the window tree. It was trapped, but still it made a pattern on the stucco and sky. A gray bird landed on a branch, turned from side to side pecking and chirping, then flew off. Her body wanted that — something to come to her. Mark had. It had liked what he did. She touched herself, imagining him leaning over her. No, he wasn't what her body wanted; she could do it herself.

The sun on her eyelids; her hand far away, moving. Suzanne rode on a lion in the desert; she wore a blue robe like Mary's. The world darkened to brown. Anne rocked deeper. All around her the yellow straw sent out sparks. Suzanne leaned over her. "My baby, my good girl." Her hand touched her cheek; the straw blazed up. Anne's body clenched and night poured through her, a river of flaming dreams.

    Later she was surprised to see light pressing into the crevices of the room. Where she'd been was so dark and deep it should have carried the world into night. She glanced around cautiously, looking for a place to lodge herself. Some shadow in the far corner. Shelter there. She saw the crèche: Joseph, Mary, the empty crib for her to crawl into. The straw pricked her back, then she sank into its softness. Warm. She reached her arms to Mary. But her mother was a statue. She needed someone else.

Suzanne. To lift her, hold her, pin the halo on her curly hair.

She lay there helpless, not knowing how to bring her, then realized she was big and could call her on the phone. She was surprised to find her body on the couch, her skin exposed to the light. She rose awkwardly, teetering on her large legs. She knew the number; it had lots of fives and sevens. "Hello," Suzanne's voice answered, and Anne said "Suzanne," but it went on talking, a mockery of a voice that couldn't hear her.

Anne hung up, feeling panic. But she knew how to do this. She called again, waited for the fake voice to finish speaking and beep. "Suzanne," she said, "I need you to come here. I don't want Mark; I want you." She paused, then rushed on, expecting her time to run out. "It's very important. I'll wait here. I need you soon. I'll wait; I won't go out. Call me right away."

Then she was sleepy. She wanted to climb back into the manger but couldn't find it. Her bed instead. She took the phone with her. The bed was still unmade, the sheets tumbled. She had been there with Mark. She looked down at her rough pale skin and saw she didn't have to get undressed. She fell onto the bed, wrapping the sheets around her.

No sun in the room. Almost evening. She sat up. So late? Why hadn't Suzanne called?

The phone had fallen. She crouched down to it. Toppling. The phone a hole in the floor. Then the world righted itself. Her hand dialed the number. She spoke angrily to the fake voice, "I told you to call right away. It's so late. Why aren't you home? What are you doing? Why did you leave me all alone?"

She waited for the answer. A buzzing and the beep. Suzanne couldn't do this. A mother wasn't allowed to leave a child this way. She could die. And then her parents would be sorry.

Her hand flung the phone across the room. It lay on its side, then shrilled at her. Her body would get her whatever she wanted.

She sprang up. She'd go to Suzanne. Take the BART and look for a house with a garden. She rushed down the stairs; the front door bumped back, then swung open again behind her. She ran in the middle of the street, empty and dark except for the haloes around the lamps. The wind sailed by her. She was about to fly, wafted up into the moist night air. She would drift over the bay, circle the city, swoop into the garden, and find Suzanne.

Something wet pulled at her foot. She sprawled on the street in a pile of damp leaves. Had she broken a leg falling? She stretched one. The other. It moved too but leaves stuck to it. She brushed them off. More, dark and wet, sticking to her hand, her shin. Liquid. Leaves' blood. No, hers.

She stood. Nothing buckled or swayed. She walked slowly home, the blood trickling down her shin. She noticed the road was rough and cold under her bare feet. She shivered; there were goose bumps on her arms and legs. She'd find Suzanne tomorrow.

When she woke in the morning, she sat on the edge of the bed and examined her legs. Dried blood crusted on her shin. She found stains on the sheets. Mommy hated it when she got things dirty. Suzanne wouldn't mind.

This time Suzanne's phone sang three notes. The fake voice wasn't hers: "The number you have reached has been disconnected, and there is no new number."

Gone. How would Anne find her now? She laid her head on her knee, wanting to rock again into nothing. But the scab on her leg distracted her; she picked at it, watched the blood drip onto the floor. She wouldn't give up this time. Her body would figure it out.

"Body, what do you know?"

"Sweetness, a stone, a hole, and flying."

"Can you find her?

"I can do anything."

"Where should I go first?"

"Mark was the beginning."

Mark would know where to find Suzanne.

Then she was very busy. It was like getting ready for school. She washed away the blood, but more kept coming, so she covered the spot with two band-aids. Next she dressed, choosing a blue skirt and a white blouse. She put money in her purse for the BART train, then added three tissues, another band-aid, and a handful of candies. She wrote the address and phone number of Mark's office on a piece of paper and put that in too. Her long black coat. She was ready; she wasn't going to be late.

So many people were lined up on the platform.

Anne was one of them; her body had disguised her; she had everything but a briefcase. She didn't mind standing with the others, letting her body sway and bump against the bodies around her. She liked it when the train pulled into a station, the momentum pushing her first back, then forward. She exaggerated the jolt, her hips jamming into the man in front of her. This was better than the school bus. Nobody knew her; she could do anything she wanted.

Montgomery Station. She stepped into wind and sunlight, the glass buildings swaying above her. She took out the slip of paper from her purse, examined it, recognized a street, walked down it into shade, found the number, and pushed open the heavy glass door.

It was like flying in the elevator. On his floor she gave her name to the receptionist, who spoke into the telephone, "Mr. Shapiro, a Miss Bloch is here to see you," then turned back to Anne. "He'll be out soon. Why don't you have a seat."

She fidgeted in the big chair, pulling at a thread in the cuff of her blouse, then holding out her legs to study them in the skirt. She pushed down one white knee sock to check her cut, pulled the bot-

tom band-aid away, and watched the blood trickle. It slid to the ribbing of her sock, pooled there,
then slowly soaked in, the wool staining red.

Mark stood above her, his head wobbling on
top of his tall body. She pulled away from him. He
looked unsteady again, a precarious structure of
blocks piled haphazardly one on top of the other
by a child too short to see the top. "You're a mess;
let's get out of here."

He hustled her into the elevator. When it
started down, she rose, floating toward the gold
ceiling. She ducked, but drifted down before she
hit her head.

"There's a place down the street," Mark told
her. He pushed her into a dark narrow coffee
shop with five booths and a counter. It smelled of
grease and disinfectant. He deposited her in the
back booth. "A coffee and a tea," he called to the
waitress.

"Put your leg up on the seat," he ordered Anne,
then held a wad of napkins against her skin and
pressed down for a minute. "I think it's stopped
bleeding. Keep it elevated."

He slid into the bench opposite her. "What
happened?"

"I picked a scab."

"Pretty big scab." He said nothing for a while, then, "Well, what do you want?"

"Where's Suzanne?"

"Drop this Suzanne shit, will you?" He rose.

"No, sit down. You've got to tell me where she lives."

He loomed over her, his head wagging wildly on its narrow neck. "Look, I've got to get back to work. Goodbye." The word broke into pieces and fell on the Formica between them. He slapped a couple of dollars on the table and strode out. *As the door swung closed behind him, his head snapped off and rolled down the fiery pavement, dissolving in the light.*

Anne followed. It felt like flying weather, the world light, airy. Her feet rose a yard from the ground, she hovered, then shot away from the sidewalk, clearing the awning of the restaurant and speeding past the rows of windows. As she twisted to look around her, one shoe fell. She kicked the other off. She bobbed near the top of the building, a granite ledge stained with pigeon droppings close enough to touch.

She wouldn't find Suzanne here. She had to get above the skyscrapers. She circled. North, the Golden

Gate and Mt. Tamalpais. The bay specked with boats to the east, the ridges with houses. In the west hills she couldn't see over. Smaller houses, dark clumps of trees, patches of bright green like handkerchiefs spread to the south. There.

But she hung, swaying in a slight breeze, unable to propel herself forward. She kicked, punched the air. Stalled. Above everything. The buildings pointed at her. Flags drooped from the tops of some. Nothing grew there. She swung in her skirt like a bell over this barrenness, and everywhere around her green beckoned, gardens she couldn't get to.

Then someone shoved her back. The flags snapped up and she sailed over the buildings west and south toward the sun. Now she was flying steadily like a ship streaming out toward the horizon. She rose higher; the buildings were so far below she made out only jagged gray rooftops. The sun pressed down on her like a hand, the glare all around her, a solid wall that parted for her and closed behind her seamlessly as she passed. She was hot. She struggled out of one arm of her coat, then carefully shifted her purse to shake out of the other. Her coat drifted down like a giant raven, sleeves flung out behind, holding onto the air.

Time seemed suspended. She never stopped, but her

pace was slow. Light rippled by her, heating up. She unzipped and wriggled out of her skirt. As she watched it
swing downward, she saw she had passed the skyscrapers. Chunky buildings topped with billboards glided
beneath her; cars stopped and started at lights or filled
parking lots. No gardens yet, but rows of trees lined
some streets and there was more space. She hung in
an enormous block of light, which carried her forward.
Its heat washed over her body. Balancing her purse,
she stripped off everything that came between her and
the sun. Her skin warmed; she looked down and saw it
glowed, and there, far below, just ahead, a rectangle of
green, a garden.

 The light that flanked her let her drop gently with a
rustling sound like a folding of wings. She landed not
in the garden but before it, in front of a small structure
with a carved and arched wooden door. To the side a
smaller door stood open. Hands pushed her forward.
This was where she'd find her. She rushed through an
entryway filled with whispering into the main building. Dark at first, pulsating. Pale lightning zigzagged
along the ceiling. The yellow glass of the windows
heaved in and out, breathing. Gold winked on the
walls. The room was peopled with presences, which
leaned toward her, flourishing swords and crosses,

reaching out hands, brushing her with their wings. As Anne's eyes adjusted, she saw on the far wall another arched door that echoed the one behind her. But it was larger, covering the entire wall, a door to the sky, glinting with gold, more ornately carved, with niches where five figures stood. And there she was to the left of the cross, her hands clasped in prayer, her crown gleaming, wind ruffling her blue robe. Around her the others gestured, lamenting, beckoning Anne or warding her off. But Mary was calm, unmoving, her face serene.

Anne ran past rows of rippling pews. She stumbled up two steps, and that motion pushed her into the air, enough so she cleared the red velvet rope and landed on a small wooden stool in front of the Virgin.

She reached to clasp the Virgin's feet, disturbing three cherubs' heads which flew away toward the ceiling. "You are my mother."

"Yes," Mary nodded, laying one long hand on Anne's head.

"It took so long to find you," Anne complained.

"I always fly with you."

Anne didn't want to be angry any more. She was safe. She climbed to a small ledge, burrowed her head into her mother's blue robe, then looked up. "It doesn't matter that I'm half Jewish?"

Mary put her hands on Anne's shoulders, holding her closer. "You're my child. You'll always be my child."

Anne wept, snuggling into the blue cloth, feeling the thighs beneath it, the damp smell of tears, of crotch, of mother. Mary stroked her hair, her forehead, her neck. "Come now; it's time to go." Her mother's hands cupped her shoulders, pulling her up. The door to the sky swung open, and they sailed into the blue.

Suzanne

When the phone rang, Suzanne let the voicemail answer. She didn't think Mark would be so stupid as to give Anne the new number she'd left with Adele, but he'd surprised her so often lately, she couldn't count on it. "Suzanne, this is Mark."

He was finally deigning to call her. Probably complaining about his car. She felt an urge to ignore him but decided she might as well get it over with. She lifted the receiver. "Hello."

"Did the police call you?"

What? He'd involved the police about a lousy tail light? "What for?"

"Did they call you about Anne?"

"Mark, I don't know what's going on. No one called me."

"They called me."

"What about?"

"Anne. They found her naked in Mission Dolores, hugging a statue of the Virgin Mary. They say she won't talk to them. My number was in her purse."

Oh God. She'd known it. Poor thing, she thought simultaneously with, it serves him right, and, thank God I'm not involved. She was careful that her reactions didn't show. "I'm sorry to hear that. But why would they call me?"

"She was looking for you. She came to see me at work to ask where you were."

"I hope you didn't tell her."

"I didn't. But don't you want to help her?"

"I don't see how I can. I don't see what this has to do with me."

"So you're denying any responsibility?" Mark's voice was harsh.

"Mark, how can I be responsible?"

"You're the one she was looking for."

"You're crazy. She's your girlfriend. You picked a basket case and drove her over the edge."

"Fuck you."

"Fuck you too. What's wrong with you? What kind of person are you taking advantage of someone like that and ruining her life and our marriage too? I thought you had some integrity. I guess I was wrong." The phone clicked off, and Suzanne held it to her ear for a moment listening to the silence, then placed it down. How could he say she was responsible? It was ridiculous. She strode out onto the patio, she needed to cut something.

The wind whipped the long branches of the butterfly bush back and forth. How had that thing gotten so big? It seemed to have shot up overnight. She reached for a waving stem and clipped it carefully above a circlet of leaves. The next one blew out of reach, so she waited for it to head back, gripped it firmly, and snipped. Damn, she'd cut her finger. She was startled to see blood seeping onto her palm. She better take care of it. Blood spilled into the bathroom sink as she put on a band aid, which was soaked almost immediately. She added a second and a third, but that didn't work, and soon there were red splotches all over. She held three cotton balls against her bleeding finger, pressed them down with her thumb, and searched in the drawer with her other hand for adhesive tape, then wound it around the cotton. Her finger throbbed. Dizzy, she stumbled to the couch and flung herself onto it. A sob shook her, then another. She couldn't remember crying this hard, not since she was a child. It went on for a long time.

When it subsided, she lay still. The cut had frightened her; that was it. It reminded her of when Carol had whittled with the Swiss army knife they weren't allowed to use without their parents' supervision. Her scream had brought Suzanne, who'd been left in charge. But when Carol had seen her, she'd panicked and run away shouting "Don't tell Mommy and Daddy," blood pouring from her finger.

How had they stopped the bleeding then? She didn't know. All she could remember was her sister dashing away from her across the lawn, Kenny muttering "dumb girl" and going back to gluing his model airplane, and her own helplessness and fear.

She was always the one who took care of everyone else. Mark would have known what to do about the cut. He fussed over any little scrape. How could he not have known there was something wrong with Anne? Fourteen years, she thought, and I never really understood him. Their marriage was over. She knew that now.

She sat stiffly and poked at the bandage. No more blood. She went out to turn off the soaker hoses. When she bent toward the metal faucet, she felt again the certainty that it was over and imagined herself old, white-haired, carrying a bag of groceries up the steps with a sure-footed, bow-legged walk like a goat's. And as she looked over her lesson plans at her desk, she felt how quiet the house was, how she would go to bed alone. "Anne went crazy," she said aloud. "Mark drove her crazy." Where was Anne now, she wondered.

She pushed away the papers. Time for bed. She sleepily moved through brushing her teeth, washing her face. She shifted under the covers, warming the sheets. She thought she might cry again, but when she lay still, she felt lifted, floating into the air. She danced with a slight olive-skinned man, his face near hers, mouthing the words to the music. His long eyelashes brushed her forehead. She wore a red dress with a full skirt. It whirled around her thighs as they circled the room.

The next day the alarm didn't wake her. Had she forgotten to set it? She hurried to get ready for work. But she found herself stopped, standing with a carton of milk in her hand, her mind for a moment elsewhere.

At school when the kids painted, she was drawn to Jesse's picture: seaweed and fish against a bright, clear blue. It felt like a window into a forgotten, familiar world. "Mrs. Shapiro," Jenny, her new aide, interrupted her. But she wasn't Mrs. Shapiro any longer.

"Just call me Suzanne," she answered.

At the end of the school day Michael waved to her across the parking lot. "Hey Suzanne," he called, "I like that color on you."

"Huh?" She looked down at her jeans and the sweatshirt she'd pulled on at the last minute, the only one that wasn't in the laundry basket. It was a Christmas present Carol had sent, a bright green she didn't usually wear. "Really?"

Michael loped over, his long hair flopping into his face. "Yeah, you look like a daisy on a stem."

Suzanne never knew how to respond to such lines. She started to say, "Don't be silly," but changed it to a prim "Thank you," remembering her grandmother's lectures on compliments.

"Wanna go for a cup of coffee? There's a new place on Mission and Twenty Third."

"Oh, no thanks." He looked so forlorn that she thought, oh well, it wouldn't hurt to be a little friendly, to convert herself from a crush to the older woman confidante. "Another time, maybe. I have to get home today."

He brightened. "O.K., great. See you tomorrow."

But when she got into her car, she realized, embarrassed by her lie, that she didn't want to go home yet. She glanced in the rear-view mirror, saw that Michael had left, then twisted the mirror, leaning back so she could see her face and the top of the sweatshirt, and studied herself. Yes, the green did look good on her, though it made her eyes less blue, more gray. But what was wrong with gray? A blue-eyed blond — what a cliché; Mark's perfect shiksa who broke his mother's heart. A gray-eyed woman in green; it sounded more mature, less like a cheerleader.

She pushed the mirror back in place and started the car. I'll drive through the park, she decided, see if anything new is blooming. And when she got home, she'd call Linda; she could tell her how to file for a divorce.

There, she had decided. She hadn't even had to think it over. It surprised her, but she knew it was what she would do.

Three weeks later she stood in the lobby of Mark's building, arranging the divorce papers in their folder. She was serving them herself. Otherwise it was too easy for him; this should feel real. In the elevator to his office, she thought of Anne. Had she been here, gliding against gravity to her lover? How could Suzanne ever have chosen someone who would betray her like that? How could she ever have loved him?

She punched the button to go down again because she was crying. She had loved him. And it didn't make the slightest bit of difference.

She rode up and down until she was in control of herself, then searched in her pockets for a tissue to wipe her face and finally had to use her sleeve. By the time she got off at his floor, she was able to calmly greet Adele, who left her desk to usher her in as though she, at least, understood the importance of what they were doing.

Then she stood in front of Mark. He rose to meet her. She remembered he was six foot one, and his curly hair was stiff to the touch. She knew him; she would always know him. He didn't beg her to change her mind. He gestured her to a seat. "So I sign these, and then your lawyer will call me?"

Suzanne nodded.

As she watched him read the papers, a frown of concentration on his face, she felt the motion of the elevator. Mark receded, getting smaller and smaller. She touched the edge of the desk. Mark read, twisting his pen between his fingers. But when she lowered her eyes, she could see it again: Mark sliding away from her, her hand on his desk empty, held open in front of her.

Had he ever been real to her, she wondered.

Mark signed the last page with a flourish. "So that's it, then." He rose and stepped toward the door as though leading her out.

"That's it." She stood too. How could he not feel anything? "Well, goodbye," she told him.

"Goodbye."

She walked out, passing Adele, who glanced

up from her phone call, and stood in the corridor, but she didn't want to take the elevator yet. She walked along the carpeted hallway. At the end she stood by the sealed window, looking out.

She stepped forward, pressing her hands against the rectangle of glass. It was cold. She felt the chill seep into her palms. There was something good about the feeling. She remembered the day Mark had said he wanted a divorce and she'd found out about Anne — the hot water on her hands and the smell of the orange peel. She saw a speck on the metal frame. She pulled her hands away from the glass to touch it, rubbing a fingertip over a slightly greasy raised surface. She scratched it with her fingernail, and most of it came off. Now there was a smudge under her nail like dirt from gardening. She wanted to get back to earth, to finish clearing the spot for the new vegetable patch. She turned and walked down the corridor. She stood in front of the elevator, reached her arm out slowly as though pushing it through water and pressed the button marked down.

Acknowledgments

Slightly different versions of the following stories have been previously published: "Mail" in *Love Stories by New Women* (Red Clay Books, reprinted by Avon Books); "A Treasure" in *Believing Everything* (Holy Cow! Press); "Women and Men" in *Colorado State Review*; "Releasing" in *What's a Nice Girl Like You Doing in a Relationship Like This?* (The Crossing Press); "Since I Fell for You" from "Women in Jazz" in *Breaking Up Is Hard To Do* (The Crossing Press); the complete "Women in Jazz" in *Barnabe Mountain Review*; and "Conspirators" in *Fiction Attic*.

I would like to thank the following people for invaluable help and support: "The group," who have given me encouragement, the best editing possible, and the wisest suggestions for decades — Ellery Akers, Gerald Fleming, the late Bill

Edmondson, and the late Peter Kunz — I couldn't have written this without you; brilliant poet and oldest friend Cathy Colman; my many other loving and supportive friends; the students, faculty, and staff of California College of the Arts, who give me a place to work that inspires and nurtures me; and the wonderful people at Black Spring Press Group, especially Dr. Todd Swift; my extremely skilled and astute editor, Dr. Memory Pinchbeck; and the always kind and helpful Amira Ghanim. And I have endless gratitude and love for my late family: my husband Herbert Yee, my sister Joan Serin, and my parents Bernard and Bernice Serin, scientists who taught me to love literature.

Judith Serin's collection of poetry, *Hiding in the World*, was published by Diane di Prima's Eidolon Editions, and her *Days Without (Sky): A Poem Tarot*, seventy-eight short prose poems in the form of a tarot deck with illustration and book art design by Nikki Thompson, was published by Deconstructed Artichoke Press. She writes fiction and creative nonfiction as well as poetry, and her work has appeared in numerous magazines and anthologies. She teaches literature and writing at California College of the Arts.